Praise for *Isn't It Romantic?*

"*Isn't It Romantic?* zips along like a Preston Sturges movie
. . . the sentences are swift and he punctuates them with a
dry wit and some genuinely droll ripostes. . . . The tiny
town of Seldom is truly a funny place."
—*New York Times Book Review*

"Ron Hansen's *Isn't It Romantic?* is a lively, affectionate,
and often poetic romp. It made me laugh out loud."
—Bob Kerrey, president of the New School University
and former Nebraska governor and senator

"A treat. . . . [*Isn't It Romantic?*] has both sophisticated and
down-homey humor . . . with laugh-out-loud scenes."
—*People*

"Hilarious . . . be prepared to be unexpectedly charmed,
delighted, and touched." —*Charlotte Observer*

"Hansen makes it fresh, crafting a tale that reads like gold
and unfolds like a laugh-out-loud film. . . . *Isn't It
Romantic?* lives up to the airy promise of its title and
delights while doing so." —*Minneapolis Star Tribune*

"Ron Hansen . . . has given us the gift of well-wrought fun
in *Isn't It Romantic?* . . . full of all the romance, confusion,
and poetry that comes when sophistication meets true salt-
of-the-earth charm." —*BookPage*

About the Author

RON HANSEN is the author, most recently, of *A Stay Against Confusion: Essays on Faith and Fiction* and of the novel *Hitler's Niece*. His previous novel, *Atticus,* was a National Book Award finalist. His other highly praised works of fiction include *Mariette in Ecstasy, The Assassination of Jesse James by the Coward Robert Ford, Desperadoes,* and the story collection *Nebraska*. With Jim Shepard, he edited the anthology *You've Got to Read This: Contemporary American Writers Introduce Stories That Held Them in Awe.* Ron Hansen is married to the novelist Bo Caldwell and lives in northern California, where he teaches fiction writing and literature at Santa Clara University.

ALSO BY RON HANSEN

FICTION

Hitler's Niece

Atticus

Mariette in Ecstasy

Nebraska

The Assassination of Jesse James by the Coward Robert Ford

Desperadoes

ESSAYS

A Stay Against Confusion: Essays on Faith and Fiction

FOR CHILDREN

The Shadowmaker

EDITOR

You've Got to Read This:
Contemporary American Writers Introduce Stories
That Held Them in Awe (with Jim Shepard)

You Don't Know What Love Is:
Contemporary American Short Stories

ISN'T IT ROMANTIC?

An Entertainment

RON HANSEN

Perennial
An Imprint of HarperCollins*Publishers*

A hardcover edition of this book was published in 2003 by HarperCollins Publishers.

First Perennial edition published 2004.

Designed by Joseph Rutt

The Library of Congress has catalogued the hardcover edition as follows:
Hansen, Ron.
    Isn't It Romantic? : an entertainment / Ron Hansen.—1st ed.
      p. cm.
    ISBN 0-06-051766-2
      1. French—Nebraska—Fiction. 2. Travelers—Fiction. 3. Nebraska—
Fiction. I. Title.

PS3558.A5133 I75 2003
813'.54—dc21

                                                                2002069082

ISBN 0-06-051767-0 (pbk.)

04 05 06 07 08 ❖/RRD 10 9 8 7 6 5 4 3 2 1

for Bo

1

America was Natalie's idea.

She'd gone to the upstairs travel agency of Madame Dubray on rue Saint-Jacques in Paris, and politely listened as Madame extolled the fresh sea oysters of Saint-Malo, the forests and glades of Perpignan where there were no longer lions, the sunstruck beaches of the Côte d'Azur where Mademoiselle could air her still-youthful breasts in innocent, unfettered freedom.

Natalie shyly hid her still-youthful breasts with her forearms as she told Madame that unfortunately those were all places that *Pierre* would have chosen for an August vacation and she was no longer interested in accommodating her shifty fiancé. She reminded Madame that she was a librarian specializing in Americana at the Bibliothèque nationale, so touring the United States seemed a more intriguing and practical choice than staying with the French in France for the August *vacances* as she'd done all her life.

Sighing, Madame agreed, in the grudging way of one who thought some people would garden in basements if you let them. "You would prefer what, Mademoiselle Clairvaux? Shopping in New York? Mickey Mouse in Orlando?"

She shook her head and said she would like to tour America on an overland route from the East Coast to the West.

Madame Dubray held her face carefully fixed as she asked, "How?"

Natalie felt unfairly tested. "Railway?"

Madame smirked. "Railway," she said. "In America."

"Or perhaps I could rent an automobile."

Madame scoffed, "Aren't you the audacious one? Motoring through all the forty states."

"There are fifty."

"Well, not worth *seeing*," said Madame.

Natalie told the travel agent that she wasn't confident there was a good way to do what she wanted, that's why she'd thought it necessary to visit Madame. But she very much wanted to see some of the attractions and natural wonders in the American interior that Europeans frequently missed. She lifted from the floor beside her a coffee-table book and turned its pages to show photographs of children on candy-striped swings below a car chase on a drive-in movie screen, snow falling on the just-alike homes of Levittown, hot sunlight and green machinery baling yellow hay in Iowa, an ominous rainstorm over a trailer park in Kansas, a girl in cowboy boots selling yard gnomes at a flea market, a giant bingo parlor with hundreds hunching over their game cards. "Like these," Natalie said, "not the typical places."

Madame Dubray gave it some thought and said, "We have one possibility."

Natalie said in English, "Oh goody!"

2

Mademoiselle Clairvaux was a gorgeous woman of twenty-six with an oval face, caramel-colored eyes, and a luxuriance of coffee-brown hair, and she sometimes wore serious eyeglasses she didn't need in order to intimidate men who seemed to think she needed touching. But she forgot those glasses in her hurried packing in Paris and she was so wearied with unsolicited attentions on the flight from Orly to New York City that she purchased heavy black spectacles like those Buddy Holly favored before she got on the Sunday morning shuttle to the Port Authority terminal.

There she found the See America bus hulking in a side

alley like a venerable but malfunctioning machine that had been cannibalized for auto parts or just plain meanness, its metal surfaces wildly paisleyed with left-over housepaints. Luggage of Samsonite, canvas, grocery box, and gunnysack was waiting to be stowed in its craw. Waiting, too, were its forlorn passengers: a crazy old coot with binoculars, some Japanese children sullenly playing with Gameboys, some Canadians for whom cordiality was not a priority, a husband and wife in matching safari jackets, a crewcut man who tip-toed wherever he went, a hugely overweight woman continually folding chocolate eclairs into her mouth, three teenaged girls from Scotland who seemed near panic over a spree that had gone lame many days ago and now considered Natalie Clairvaux with desperate affection.

She nearly walked away, but she knew such delicacy about transportation and companionship would make her a tourist, not a traveler. She'd lack moxie. And so she joined the See America tour as she'd planned.

The first stop was Hoboken and the boyhood home of Frank Sinatra, though there was no sign on the house and the owner looked worriedly at them from a chink in the venetian blinds. They then saw the world's largest buffet; the location for a 1940s movie that starred either Peter Lorre or Adolphe Menjou; a café where a waitress succeeded in juggling four out of five coffee cups; Punxsatawney, Pennsylvania, where on February second a woodchuck seeing or not seeing its shadow would somehow predict the climate; a hideous motel near Lake Erie where the tour group was put up that night, and where Mademoiselle Clairvaux hesitated at her room's threshold for many minutes, skeptically staring in.

In eastern Ohio, Natalie woke up from a morning nap in a truckstop where idling semis throbbed and percolated outside the bus windows. Huddling like a waif, she walked down a long line of them, considering with puzzlement the opportunities that a number of truckers offered, and found her tour group inside a cafeteria. She herded along behind them, skating a tray on aluminum rails, and choosing from among the appalling alternatives some crusty chicken pieces. A cook then plopped a softball of mashed potatoes on Natalie's dish and flooded the plate with Crayola-yellow gravy. The husband in the safari jacket confided, "We're packing beef jerky if you need it."

She had no idea what that was.

The husband was about to show her when his wife began hitting him with a spoon.

The next stop was the House of Bottles, and then Heine's Place where they all glumly peered at an orange ten-ton wheel of cheese in a refrigerated glass case. A sign on the wall said CHEDDAR. In Akron they tentatively entered an exhibit hall underneath a sign that read GOODYEAR'S WORLD OF RUBBER. Indiana was introduced by a pharmacist who gave his interpretation of the name "Hoosier," held up for all to see the hand that shook the hand of Larry Bird, and guided them through the James Dean Grave and Memorial where Natalie counted three of the late actor's imitators slouching through the cemetery in blond ducktails, black motorcycle jackets, and dangling cigarettes.

In Illinois there was an overnight at an even worse motel and from the room next door the continual ouching sounds of two salesmen snapping towels at each other while a bathtub filled. In Chicago's stockyards they squeezed inside an old hog pen for a recitation of a poem by someone named Sandburg, then they visited a piano tuner, chewed gum outside Wrigley Field, watched sheets of children's arithmetic homework swirl down the streets of the Windy City, and strolled through fields of broom corn in Arcola.

There was a tour of Herbert Hoover's birthplace in West Branch, Iowa; Coca-Cola and celery sticks at the home of the grandmother who won the Tiniest Handwriting Contest; a visit to the spick-and-span headquarters of

Maytag Appliances in Newton; and to a Chevrolet dealership in Council Bluffs where each member of the group got
to sit with a salesman and haggle over the price of an
Impala.

In Omaha's Red Lion Inn Wednesday morning, Natalie
sat with an Englishman named Clive at breakfast and said,
"I am so excited to be here."

Clive slurped his tea as she smiled at him, then solemnly
resettled the cup in its saucer. "Compulsory politeness com-
pels me to ask why."

She told him she was born in the city of Rouen but
she'd grown up in the Hôtel de La Manche that her grandmother owned in Port-en-Bessin on the shore of the English
Channel, not far from the area that on D-Day, June 6, 1944,
was known as Omaha Beach.

"And here we are in Omaha now," Clive said. "So this
wasn't an impertinence on your part."

She told him Madame Sophie Clairvaux had been sev-
enteen in 1944 and when she met some of the soldiers with
the 352nd Division she thought of them all as movie stars.
She was sure she'd seen Gary Cooper striding dourly in a
rainstorm. She was confident it was Clark Gable who'd
winked at her from the front seat of a Jeep. And she'd fallen
in love with a sergeant named Mitch who taught the French

girl what a French kiss was, then left with his battalion the next morning. Sophie never heard from him again. She presumed he'd been killed. But she remembered him frequently, and even after a lifetime of hearing American tourists gripe about cold bath water, signs not written in English, and the constant noisiness of the sea, Madame Clairvaux was still wildly passionate about all things American, and she passed that along to Natalie.

"Would you mind terribly if I took advantage of your toast?" Clive asked.

She handed him the plate and told him she was three when she first used the English word "actually" in a sentence. At eight she'd memorized the lyrics to Ella Fitzgerald's "I Got It Bad (and That Ain't Good)." She requested, and got, a subscription to *Mad* magazine on her thirteenth birthday, and sorely wanted to go to America for college, but Madame Sophie Clairvaux so wanted her closer to Normandy that Natalie attended the Sorbonne, studying English literature, collecting old copies of *Photoplay*, and living in a garret near the cathedral of Notre Dame with ceilings so low she was forced to stoop as she cooked, and with walls so thin that she swore she could hear the optometrist next door swallow as she watched *Little House on the Prairie*. Then she earned a master's degree in library science and went to work at the Bibliothèque nationale, where she met Pierre Smith at a party, told him he resembled a blond Rams linebacker, and was forced to explain "Rams" and "linebacker" and whether the man he resembled was preposterously handsome. And Pierre was so manly, charming, smart, and attractive that by evening's end she'd discovered she'd got it bad for him.

"And that ain't good?" Clive asked.

She shrugged.

Clive asked whilst chewing her toast, "Would this panting chap be he?"

She turned. Striding in high dudgeon across the floor of the Red Lion Inn was indeed her fiancé, his beautiful tie and black Italian suit tortured by air and railway travel, his blond lion's mane in wild turmoil, his face aflame with shock and seriousness and the sunburn of insult. When he achieved their booth, he skewered her with a cold blue stare as he flung out his right arm and an index finger of accusation that seemed to guarantee an immediate "Ah hah!"

"Ah *hah*!" Pierre cried.

She turned back to Clive. "Yes. It's him."

3

Waiting on the sidewalk near the See America bus with the over-interested tour group, Pierre told Natalie in French that he'd been frantic about her disappearance until he finally recalled the name of the travel agent she'd used for her Brontë Sisters Weekend and got Natalie's itinerary from Madame Dubray just yesterday morning. She'd got him on the next flight from Paris to Chicago and the overnight Amtrak into Omaha.

She imitated Madame. "Railway. In America?"

"Madame is as crazy as you are. She told me planes do

not fly to Omaha. She said this while she watered her plants. And then she watered my head."

With a meaningful glare, Natalie said, "She knew."

"Ariel? That was just a kiss! On her birthday!"

"And Isabelle?"

"Weeks and weeks ago, before we were engaged."

"And that girl in the Luxembourg Gardens?"

"But I'm French!"

"You're English."

"A hundred years ago! And only on my grandfather's side of the family!"

"So you're a mere product of your socialization in the city of romance."

"Through and through! It's like an illness!" A hand raked back his wild blond hair as he shook his head in shame. "Oh," he moaned, "how I wish there were a cure!"

The crazy old coot with binoculars asked in English, "Are you two speaking Spanish?"

Pierre glowered and flicked a hand at him, and he scurried.

Natalie asked, "Are you intending to join me now?"

"I have a ticket."

"We'll share the bus. That is all."

The hydraulic doors of the See America bus shushed open and people commenced pushing inside as if sale prices had been slashed. And for the first time Pierre observed the group he'd be joining on their tour, seeing a guy dribble the last of his Coca-Cola on the sidewalk and then smash the empty can against his forehead. Pierre turned to his fiancée and objected in French, "But they are *peasants*!"

With irritation she shoved ahead of him and got into a window seat near the front of the bus, shifting away from Pierre when he took the aisle seat next to her. Two high school boys in street clothes got on with scuba masks and fins in their hands and scuba tanks on their backs. An enormous man who'd joined the tour in Cleveland huffed after the boys, carrying a long something that was wetly dripping through its butcher paper wrapping. Clive averted his eyes as he sidled down the aisle. And then there was an old shawled woman towing along a son in his fifties whose name tag read "Seymour" and who was holding a plastic bag with a goldfish floating in it. They were followed by a hugely overweight woman in a raccoon coat with a cake box in her hands. She squinted at Pierre and his aisle seat and with annoyance said, "You. Skedaddle."

Pierre glanced up, "*Quoi, Madame?*" (Pardon me?)

"Don't start with me."

Helplessly looking to Natalie, he asked, "*Qu'est-ce qu'elle dit?*" (What's she saying?)

The woman with the cake box informed him, "I am not the milk of human kindness!"

Natalie told Pierre in English, "She is not milk." And then she looked out the window again.

Sheepishly getting up, Pierre headed down the aisle, and the woman haughtily sat, saying to Natalie as she opened the cake box, "And you can just keep your hands to yourself." She then lifted out a three-layer coconut cake that she held up in front of her mouth like a sandwich. She took a bite and coconut flakes snowed down her front.

Scanning the seats behind her, Natalie found her fiancé huddled down in the rearmost booth seat and squeezed between the old shawled woman and the son with the gold-fish. As the tour bus rolled forward, he looked plaintively at her as if he were a schoolchild being unjustly punished.

She smiled.

4

Much later on a gray two-lane highway that was branched with tar, she looked over her shoulder to find her dolorous fiancé cradling the plastic bag of goldfish in his lap as Seymour held out a Nebraska road map and prattled on about sites. Sympathetically, she wrestled past the fat woman and walked back to Pierre.

Seymour was saying, "Another roadside attraction you'll want to show your girlfriend is Harold Warp's Pioneer Village. About twenty miles southeast of Kearney. In Minden, Nebraska. Two of my favorite displays are the monkey wrench exhibit in the agricultural building and a living diorama of all seven native Nebraska grasses. Warp, as you may know, made his loot in Chicago, with plastics. Flex-O-Glass, Glass-O-Net, and Red-O-Tex. If you haven't heard of any of them, then you're obviously not a Midwestern chicken farmer."

Pierre seemed sunken and yoked with a great weight as he eyed Natalie pensively and said, "*On a besoin de parler.*" (We need to talk.)

"We are in America," she said. "We should speak English."

He got a mimeographed sheet of paper from inside his suit coat and shook it. "It is that I have read at last now our itinerary. Look at how we shall be eatings. Look at where we sleeps. What is cooking in your head?" He rattled the sheet again and scanned it. "We are to introduce ourselves to 'Little Miss Middle-of-Nowhere.' And then corn detasseling, whatever is that. We go to Chester, the birthplace of six-man football. We dine at the Wednesday night meeting of the Nebraska Catfishing Club. Are you thinking this is amusing for I?"

She'd be the first to admit her voice was teeny as she answered, "It has its charms."

"We could have gone to Avignon. But no. You do not want to go to Avignon. We could have gone to Aix. Again, you do not want to go to Aix. We are hearing good things from friends about Basel. *Mais non*, we could not go there. We had to go on . . . *un pèlerinage*!"

"A pilgrimage."

"We had to go on a *carnival* bus!"

The old shawled woman beside him patted his wrist and said, "Life is sometimes a rocky road."

And then they heard a blowout and the bus jounced violently. Natalie saw crows of tire rubber flying onto the highway, and then she saw Pierre scowling up at her.

"*C'est un complot*," he said. (This is a plot.)

5

They were stalled in an out-of-the-way section of Nebraska prairie where, as some citizens put it, the east and west peter out. Waving grasses, hot zephyrs in the mid-eighties, a certain crankiness to the trees, skies of a Windex blue. Worried and impatient tourists were milling about outside the bus or lounging dissolutely on their luggage, and the See America driver was hunched next to a rear wheel well, his hands on his knees, trying to fix the flat just by staring at it.

Waiting tranquilly on a hillside of wildflowers, a red suitcase on rollers beside her, Natalie tilted her head back against a cattle fence so her face could catch the noontime sun as Pierre scrupulously examined the sleeves and cuffs of his Italian suit and cursed each time he picked a sticker or cocklebur from it. Wide Hereford cows were six feet away, their ears twitching tenacious flies, their mouths moving sideways as they chewed, their soft brown eyes watching him without curiosity. "Look at my clothings," he said. "We are supposed to be on the happy vacation, but instead one is being addicted."

"Afflicted."

"*Oui.*"

"And last August?"

Pierre loomed gigantically over her but there was a littleness to him as he evaluated whether this were a trick question. Without certainty he answered, "Cap d'Antibes."

"In Cap d'Antibes you stared at everyone's breasts but mine."

"Yours always had books over them."

"In Saint Laurent you took those long walks. Alone."

"How many times can you watch *Shame*?"

"*Shane*," Natalie corrected.

"Cowboys," he said, and made a gun of his hand. "Bang bang."

"In Strasbourg . . . ," she said.

". . . you are in the library all the times."

She looked at him with sarcasm. "Perhaps I was researching the problem of male lust."

Pierre was stumped. "What is this word loost?"

"*Plein de désir sexuel*."

"Well, that is the difference between us. You research; I . . . *fais des expériences*?"

"Experiment."

"*C'est juste*. I experiment."

"And what does one do when the experiment is over?"

Each considered the other for a long time. In a city far away someone dropped a pin.

"Today is Wednesday," Natalie said.

"*Mercredi*," Pierre insisted.

"We have until Sunday to decide if we are to finally marry."

"Make it Saturday!"

Natalie got up and confidently walked down the hillside with her red wheeled suitcase in tow.

And he yelled after her, "Noon!"

She did not go toward the still-disabled See America bus but toward the shade trees, houses, and water tower of a Nebraska farm town half a mile away.

Pierre forlornly looked at the loitering passengers and

then at his fiancée, whose suitcase swerved on uneven ground and fell over. She righted it. Pierre shouted, "*Super! C'est ce qu'on appelle une aventure?*" (Great! Is this what you call an adventure?)

She didn't turn.

He shouted, "*On va rater le bus!*" (We're going to miss the bus!)

She called back, "*On prendra le prochain!*" (We'll catch the next one!)

Walking after her with his valise, Pierre yelled, "*C'est encore plus bête que de venir ici!*" (That is even more stupid than coming here in the first place!)

6

Seldom, Nebraska. Population 395.

Natalie hauled her suitcase inside the Main Street Café in one of those *Bus Stop* entrances and she was surprised to notice a sudden silence settle on the diners there, to see farmers in their feed caps turn in their pink vinyl booths and stare, and truckers rotate on their pink and chrome counter stools, as if this were a *What the hell?* moment combined with a *Lo and behold*.

She was pretty enough that they'd have taken a gander anyway, but there was that hint of the exotic, too, like she hailed from east of Omaha and would brook no questioning about it. Owen Nelson was there, though, and Dick Tupper, naturally, and locals knew they'd appoint themselves as a welcoming party, full of interrogatories and a healthy concern for the lost lady's welfare.

Natalie felt the café's interest and with some embarrassment hauled her suitcase toward a booth where she oh so primly sat.

And then Pierre entered and the stares flew to him, the force of them tilting him a little off-balance. No one failed to notice he was holding a tasseled shoe in his hand. They did not consider it much of a weapon.

Carlo Bacon, the cook, called out from the kitchen, "Since when did Seldom become a *travel* destination?"

Pierre sought out Natalie and sat down across from her in the booth, setting his fancy and ruined Ferragamo loafer between them on the Formica. With fierce accusation, he said in English, "I have torned my favorite shoe."

She ignored him.

Looking around the café above the hats of the still watching, he saw on the walls of whitewashed oak stuffed pheasants, an antlered rabbit, and old hanging heads of deer and moose that looked distraught and humorless. And next to the kitchen door was a locked gun case. His fears were confirmed. "*Regarde*," he whispered.

She did. She was horrified.

The Wednesday installment of *The Young and the Restless* went to commercial, giving Iona Christiansen an opportunity to get two iced waters and two menus. She carried them to the booth. She was a beauty, a sultry blonde of twenty-three with a disappointed pout to her mouth and those overpowering attributes of the flesh that made men feel helpless, lovelorn, and pitifully adolescent. Pierre smiled oafishly at the waitress, just like so many before him, but Iona was immune to such appraisals and merely read the shoemaker's name inside the loafer.

Pierre presumed there was a fixed price three-course meal, and said in his unpracticed English, "It is that one would like the *prix fixe*."

"The prefix?" Iona asked. "Oh, it's four oh two."

Owen helpfully supplied the data that the area code changed to 308 a little farther west.

Pierre slightly turned in Owen's direction and nodded his thanks.

"You want coffee?" Iona asked.

Pierre agreeably smiled. Iona glanced at Natalie, who put up two fingers. Pierre put up two fingers, too.

"Two then," Iona said and strolled back to the coffeemaker.

Pierre hunkered forward and said in a hushed voice, "*On va prendre racine ici.*" (We'll be stranded here.)

Natalie shrugged.

And in the booth north of them, Owen Nelson asked Dick Tupper, "Was that *French?*"

Dick lifted halfway from his seat, imitated a good stretch and yawn as he turned just so, and interestedly stared at them fuming silently in their booth. Returning to his seat, he told Owen, "Looks like they're having a tiff."

Owen tilted out of the booth to watch Iona deliver the coffee, carefully placing the saucers and cups on each side of the tasseled loafer. Sitting up again, he said, "I say the shoe's involved." A paper napkin was farmerishly stuffed under his green workshirt collar, and he patted his mouth with it. "You don't know 'em, do ya?"

"Oh now, don't go introducing yourself again."

Owen got up. "That's how I met Slim Pickens that one time."

Owen Nelson was in his thirties and a salt-of-the-earth guy whose height and girth were sufficient to make him a third-string offensive tackle for the famous University of Nebraska Cornhuskers, though he never lorded that fact over the locals but was a friend to all and sundry. Owen inherited his dearly departed father's gas station kitty-corner from the café, and townsfolk all thought the world of him, but he was frankly not much of a mechanic, so those who'd reached the age of reason generally just rented his hoist and tools.

Owen was friendliest with Dick Tupper, a purveyor of cattle whose ranch was three miles north of town and who was just lately wealthy, having sold off four hundred acres of sorghum and soybeans to an agriculture conglomerate. Dick was a fine-looking, hard-bodied, mustached man just past fifty, and the sole misery of his life was that a decade ago his perpetually unpleasant wife ran off to Idaho's Salmon River Mountains with a wildlife manager named Calvin who wanted to be a fishing guide. Thenceforth Dick lived like a widower, still feeling married and faithful and carrying on like a chilly Lord Byron in spite of the divorce she'd gotten. But his fiftieth birthday was a jolt to his system, and since then he'd been meeting flirtatious and lonesome husband-seekers in Internet chat groups and driving as far as Lincoln to share rack of lamb and I-and-Thou talk in the halo of glimmering candles. With that history as his guide, and in just a short glimpse, Dick was able to postulate that Natalie was unhappy with her hulking companion, and he too got up to introduce himself.

Pierre gloomily registered the two men's genial

approach and urgently told Natalie, "*Ne fais pas de mouvements brusques.*" (Don't make any sudden moves.)

Owen stood aside to free his workshirt of the stained paper napkin and shyly told Dick, "You go."

"Excuse me," Dick told them. "We don't mean to intrude upon your precious time here together, but we haven't seen you in these parts and I was wondering if you had some problem on the road or you had people here or just where it is you hail from."

Pierre and Natalie stared at him in silence. Eight, maybe nine seconds passed. *The Young and the Restless* was the only sound. And then Owen shouted, "Wants to know who you are!"

Dick nodded toward the gas station owner and said, "That's Owen." Extending his hand to Natalie, he said, "My name's Dick Tupper."

His hand was held out there for a moment before Natalie cautiously took it. "Natalie Clairvaux," she said.

Dick turned to *Il Penseroso* for a handshake. "Pleased to meetcha."

Pierre said with sarcasm, "Hi."

"Didn't catch your name."

Pierre smiled at Dick and said, "*Je vous déteste tous.*" (I hate you all.)

Owen asked, "Was that French you were speaking?"

Pierre, suffering, held his face in his hands. *"Mon Dieu."*

To Owen's question, Natalie nodded uncertainly, as if they'd committed a crime.

Dick smiled at Natalie and said, "Pretty language." And to Owen he said, "She could be a sister to that French actress we like."

"Which?"

"Pretty brunette, bee-stung lips. She was in that sand dune motion picture. And *Camille Claudel.*"

"Oh yeah," Owen said. "Isabelle Adjani."

Dick smiled at Natalie. "Are you kin?"

She shook her head.

Owen invited himself to join the travelers by swiveling a chair around and straddling it at their booth. "Okay," he told Dick. "We got an intricate situation here. They could be penniless and adrift and far from any kind of help, or they could be viticulturalists just traipsing hither and yon, scouring the vincyards of our fair Nebraska homeland."

They all gave Owen the look he so often deserved, bless his heart.

Dick helped out by saying, "My friend wants to know if either of you are employed in the wine trade."

Natalie answered, "Yes. *He* is."

Owen lifted his eyes heavenward. "Owe ya one, Big Husker."

"Well, this is real *seldom* for us here," Dick said.

Everyone in the café groaned.

He ignored them. "Just how long did you plan to stay?"

Pierre sourly told him, "We have miss-ed our bus."

"Owen, when's the Greyhound due next?"

With a grin, he answered, "Way afterwards."

"Are you thinking what I'm thinking?"

"We are on the same page, my friend."

Worriedly, Pierre whispered to Natalie, "*Qu'est ce qui se passe?*" (What's happening?)

She shrugged.

Watching intently from the kitchen, Carlo Bacon—whose real name was Carl—thought it high time to insert himself into the plot, and he walked out into the dining room, wiping his hands on the "Kiss the Cook" apron he wore in hopes that Iona would one day take the hint. He'd been a high school classmate of the waitress, and he hankered for her in the worst way, but he was skinny as a clarinet and toad-eyed and shrewd, with a Dick Tracy mustache and dyed black hair that he slicked back with Wildroot, and whenever he was around Iona he was so jittery that people said he made coffee nervous.

"So they're waylaid here?" he asked Owen, and Owen gave him a coded look. Carlo nodded, tilted toward Iona to confide, "I'll go get your Grandma," and then hurried outside to the three-story rooming house next door. But when he was hurtling up the front porch steps, he saw the paisley See America bus warily rolling into Seldom, all its windows filled with faces hunting the lost Europeans.

Wildly waving his arms, he jumped to the lawn and sprinted toward the tour bus, halting just in front of it. The brakes whined and a side door wheezed open as he went around to it. "Are you looking for a French couple?" Carlo asked.

With irritation the bus driver turned to his paying customers. "Were they French?"

Opinions were multiple.

"Had accents," the bus driver told him.

"Well, they've decided to stay in our Arcadian greenery for a while. The Revels and all. So: mystery solved. *Au revoir.*"

Eyeing him with suspicion, the bus driver asked, "Do they know there's no refund?"

"Oh, they're real cavalier about that."

A funk settled on the See America man as he shifted into reverse. "But they were just about to meet Little Miss Middle-of-Nowhere!"

Carlo ticked his head. "That's why it was such a thorny decision."

In the Main Street Café, Pierre heard a familiar noise of grinding gears and squeezed his face against the window to get a view south as he asked, "*Est-ce que c'était notre autocar?*" (Was that our bus?)

"*Vous le détestiez.*" (You hated it.)

"*Mais c'était avant que je ne sois venu ici.*" (But that was before I came here.)

Dick heard their fractious tones and asked, "Excuse my being so personal, but you two married?"

And Pierre said, too fiercely, "Ha!"

Natalie scorched him with her eyes. "*Ha?*"

"*Oui,*" he said. "*C'est très drôle.*" (Yes. It's very funny.)

She inched further away.

Carlo Bacon strolled back in and gave Owen a wink. "She's coming."

Owen confided to Pierre, "You'll be staying with me."

Pierre just stared at him.

With jealousy, Dick said, "I was the one first introduced myself."

"And why would he want to hole up on a cattle ranch?" Owen asked. "Anyone could tell by just looking that these are cosmopolitan people."

"So-called urbanites," said Iona.

Elderly, tottery, but grandly elegant Mrs. Marvyl Christiansen entered the café. She was seventy-five and a widow and a former high school instructor in French language and culture to a majority in the café. She was still teachy, and Owen and Dick alertly jumped up like this was homeroom and a certain protocol was expected. Owen called, "We got company from France, Marvyl!"

She smiled and seated herself in a queenly way before softly gesturing that the men could sit again. And she said in a good accent and a higher voice than normal, "*Bonjour, Mademoiselle. Bonjour, Monsieur.*"

Natalie nodded. "*Bonjour.*"

"*Comment allez-vous?*"

Iona informed the others, "She's asking them how they are."

Natalie told Mrs. Christiansen, "*Bien.*"

Iona translated. "She said she's just fine." Iona observed Pierre observing her and failed to blush with embarrassment.

Mrs. Christiansen asked, "*Comment vous appelez-vous?*"

And Iona said, "She might could be asking them who they are."

Natalie gave their names and Pierre scowled as if she were committing treachery.

Mrs. Christiansen asked, "Shall I tell them about The Revels?"

"That would be the primary option," Dick said.

Mrs. Christiansen seemed to pause to construct sentences worthy of the Académie Française, but she was confused as to vocabulary and fell back onto phrases in her high school textbooks. She asked if that was Natalie's spoon. She said her father had a splendid tailor. She said poodles were good swimmers, and there was a danger of asphyxiation in a room full of shoes.

Natalie smiled pleasantly, but Pierre leaned toward her and whispered, "*Ils sont tous fous.*" (They're all crazy.)

Closely watching the two, Dick had a hunch that his former teacher's language skills had slackened some, and Mrs. Christiansen was lost in the Ardennes forest and seeking a post office on a Sunday when Dick interrupted to say, "I hate to interrupt, ma'am, but she does speak American English."

Natalie nodded as she touched Mrs. Christiansen's wrist. "But really, you were doing quite well."

"*Merci,*" Mrs. Christiansen said. She gathered her thoughts into English and then instructed both visitors on their local custom, which was that each summer in Seldom there was a three-day festival in honor of its founder, a nineteenth-century trapper from Bordeaux whose name was Bernard LeBoeuf.

Carlo said, "It's why Nebraska used to be called The Beef State."

"Oh, foo," Iona said. "Where'd you get that?"

"Common knowledge," Carlo said. And then he got defensive and sullen for a while.

Mrs. Christiansen went on to say it was their habit to invite a visiting couple who strayed into town to be king and queen of The Revels.

Iona said of The Revels, "We have lots of parties. And fun stuff at the fairgrounds."

Dick said, "Often the royalty are carefree and footloose retirees, such as Archie and Lynette Doolittle of Detroit."

Owen grinned in reminiscence. "Claimed they were spending their children's inheritance. Wore those 'I'm With Stupid' shirts. Real comical people."

Mrs. Christiansen continued chidingly, "But they could not speak a *lick* of French."

"Oh no," Owen said, tee-heeing. "You put a shotgun to Archie's head and he could not get out a *merde*."

"Owen," Mrs. Christiansen said, and when he faced her, she put three fingers to his lips. He hushed.

"Seldom's founder was French," she went on, "so it

seems perfectly just and charming that you two should be our royalty."

"For three days?" Natalie asked.

"You will be our guests until Saturday evening."

Pierre was uncivil over the prospect and was shaking his head from side to side, but Natalie pretended not to notice as she smiled and said, "Oh goody."

Pierre's face communicated half loathing and half what-have-you-gotten-us-into?

Mrs. Christiansen sharply said, "Stop tapping your feet."

And Carlo Bacon said, "Sorry, ma'am."

Mrs. Christiansen held out both arms and Owen and Dick helped her stand. She asked, "And where is Monsieur staying?"

"With me," Owen said.

Mrs. Christiansen patted Pierre's forearm with sympathy and said, "Will you please come with me, Mademoiselle?"

7

Walking south on Main Street, Natalie watched a husband and wife in their eighties pleasantly hold hands on a front porch swing. Calliope music issued from an ice cream truck as it trolled ahead of chasing children. Two barefoot boys with bamboo poles scuffed along in the cool of the bluegrass front yards, sharing the weight of a stringer of catfish. Natalie told Mrs. Christiansen, "It is a charming village, Seldom."

"Oh my yes," Mrs. Christiansen said. "That Norman Rockwell's got nothing on us."

Mrs. Christiansen's rooming house was just next door, a

grand, three-story, Victorian affair, with a wrap-around porch and many gables, each element of carpentry differently painted in imitation of the houses she'd seen on her lone trip to San Francisco. Owen and Pierre watched from the street as Dick gallantly hefted Natalie's red suitcase from the café for her, carefully set it next to the front door, and rapidly retreated to the front lawn. Mrs. Christiansen noticed Natalie's puzzlement and explained, "We don't permit men on the premises."

Natalie smirked triumphantly at Pierre and said, "No problem." She went inside.

Owen threw his arm around his newfound pal and escorted him to his gas station across the street, saying proudly, "You got one glorious surprise in store for yourself!"

Owen's late father had not troubled himself to modernize the gas station, which was a flashback to the forties, just a one-bay garage with a hoist and oiled cinder floor and a full-service area with faded red pumps topped by white globes of illumination that had red-winged horses leaping skyward on them.

The Reverend Dante Picarazzi was there, holding a gas nozzle as he filled an old, faded Volkswagen van that had an excess of New York decals on it. He was a fast-talking priest in his forties, just a little beyond a midget in height, with crow-black hair and mustache and goatee, and without the Roman collar you'd have thought he was an East Coast movie director scouting talent or rural locations.

Owen whispered confidingly to Pierre, "You know that Paul Simon song where he sings about me and Julio down by the schoolyard?"

"I have not heard."

Owen quoted, "'When the radical priest come to get us released we was all on the cover of *Newsweek*.'" And then he surreptitiously pointed to Reverend Picarazzi. "Radical priest was him. When he first got here he was full of opinions, and now he's just like the rest of us."

Hanging up the gas hose, Dante said in a Brooklyn accent, "Owe ya a dime, Owen."

"Duly noted." Owen draped a heavy arm around Pierre and said, "My French friend here's staying with me for The Revels."

The Reverend considered him and said to Pierre, "You poor schnook." And then he got into his van.

Hanging sideways on the full-glass office door was a sign that read, THE MECHANIC IS OUT. Owen failed to change it as he walked inside. The office was filled with car batteries, hoses, and fan belts, as well as a hundred or so video tapes for rent, a hand-cranked cash register, a rack of Wrigley's chew-

RON HANSEN

ing gums, and another of air fresheners that when dangled for
some weeks in a vehicle would fractionally reveal the photos
of buxom women whose unquenched passions seemed to ren-
der them immodest. Hanging from the fluorescent ceiling
light was a sign that read, HUSKER FOOTBALL SPOKEN HERE.
Owen lifted off some cash receipts that were stabbed onto an
upended wooden block with a ten-penny nail pounded
through it. He got serious for a few seconds as he effected
arithmetic, then he shoved them inside the cash register, saying, "When I'm hither and yon, I'll let folks fill up on their
own and leave me IOUs. We have that kind of town."

Next to the video tapes was a door marked *Private* and
he motioned for Pierre to follow him as he sidestepped to it
through the high walls of clutter. With his hand on the
doorknob, Owen stopped and peered at Pierre solemnly.
"You gotta say, 'Go Big Red.'"

Pierre just stared at him.

"It's what we say in honor of our four-time national
champs. You try it now: 'Go Big Red!'"

Pierre, just mimicking, said, "Go beeg uhr-red."

"Now say, 'What game *you* watching, ref?'" But Owen
laughed and the door gave way to a bungalow attached to
the gas station.

The front room seemed furnished wholly in red blankets, bleacher cushions, jackets, banners, pens, glassware, and framed posters of the Nebraska Cornhuskers. Even the lamps and red telephone were particular to the team. Owen heaved his sizeable self down on his blanketed sofa and with fresh eyes surveyed the magnificence of what he had created there. "I just wish I could be looking at all this like you are now. I'm kinda jaded after all these years. There's fancy touches I hardly see anymore. And the thrill of a perfectly unified interior motif isn't there like it once was."

Pierre was in scan mode and unsure of his emotions. "*C'est dégueulasse,*" he said. (It's disgusting.)

Owen got up and went to a bookcase that held his many tomes on wine as well as Husker memorabilia and annuals that went back to the days when Bob Devaney so brilliantly coached. "What'd you say your surname was?" Hearing nothing from Pierre, he asked. "Pierre . . . what?"

"Smith," Pierre said.

"Are you funning me, Pete?"

"It is that we are British on my father's side."

Owen frowned like a welfare worker. "Was that a burden when you were a boy?"

Pierre shrugged and did that puffy French thing with his mouth. "They could not pronounce. I was called Smeet."

Owen seemed to get the shivers. And then he hunted up

the Smith name in his vintner's directories as Pierre fasci-
natedly wandered about the bungalow, examining the
Husker paraphernalia. Wallpaper borders bore the
Nebraska Cornhusker logo. A dining room sideboard was
filled with Husker dishware and glassware and steins. A
signed picture of Doctor Tom Osborne hung there like a
household saint. The bathroom was painted red. Pierre
switched on the light and heard the Husker theme song of
"There is no place like Nebraska" harangue him from the
overhead vent before he hurriedly switched it off. A sponge
finger gesturing that the team was #1 was on the com-
mode's flush handle and the seat cover was furred in red.
Pierre hesitantly lifted it like someone fearing the worst in a
horror movie. There was no blood, no floating head.

Owen went to another book. "Here we are. Pierre
Smith, neego-see-ant."

Walking out of the bathroom, Pierre corrected his pro-
nunciation: "*Négociant.*"

"Why, for goodness sakes, you're the WalMart of wines
over there!"

"But no. That is my big father."

"Your beeg fahzer? Oh, your *grand*father! But you're
inheriting the business, right?"

"*Peut-être.*" (Perhaps.)

Owen was all but overtaken by delirious joy. "You could not know this, but it's been my life's work and my great big impossible dream to someday chaperone my wines into the loving embrace of a fancy wine importer, and lo and behold from out of the blue comes waltzing into my life the MVP of the wholesale market!"

"Yes?"

Owen put a Budweiser football schedule marker at his name and solemnly placed the directory in his bookcase. With wet eyes he said, "I have a feeling of reverence about this occasion. I mean, what are the odds of meeting you here, now, without a handy boost from good ol' divine providence? You represent my ship coming in, Mon-sir Pierre Smith. And me? I represent the flat-out best new wine you'll ever taste."

Pierre registered that with great disbelief, and a feeling of What-else-can-go-wrong? "You are makings the wines?"

"Absolutely!"

"Here?"

"You bet!"

Pierre pointed to the floor. "In *Nebraska*?"

Owen crooked his finger in a hithering gesture and hustled out back through the kitchen and screen door to the yard while getting out his padlock key. Pierre hesitantly followed. Owen called behind him, "Experimented with sixty percent cabernet sauvignon grape and about thirty percent merlot, plus some cabernet franc and malbec to keep it true to the soft and fruity Bordelaise style." He unlocked a padlock to a root cellar whose doors were aslant at his feet. "But what I happened on by sheer accident was the petit verdot grape, which doesn't yield all that much so it's not commercially viable, but you add about five percent of that to the mix and you get surprising depth of character and a rich, reddish-black color in an otherwise fragile wine."

Pierre understood just enough to be speechless.

Owen heaved up the cellar doors and paused. "Say, 'Go Big Red!'" Pierre began, "Go . . ." but Owen elbowed him. "I was just joshing ya." He let the doors bang wide, scattering indignant insects whose only home is the grass. "My reds are big, I'll grant you," he said, "but they're also surprisingly complex, with just a hint of black currant and a strong, durable finish."

Owen and Pierre rumbled down the wooden steps to an underground root cellar that held tall racks of hundreds of bottled wines. Owen screwed an overhead sixty-watt lightbulb tight to illuminate the cellar, and Pierre considered his precise arrangements and his orderly tools and charts. At least here Owen was perfectly organized.

Pierre asked, "*Tous ces vins. . . .* Yours?"

Owen nodded. "You want a taste?"

Pierre shrugged noncommittally, like a high school kid trying to be cool. And then curiosity carried the day and he said, "Okay."

Owen went to a rack, got out a high-shouldered bottle, and proudly held it up to Pierre. "Big Red, that's our brand name. And see here on the label? Miss in boo-telly ow chat-o."

Pierre corrected, "*Mise en bouteille au château.*"

"Means I make it right here. And on the flip side," Owen said, delicately giving it a half revolution, "the complete Husker football scores for that vintage."

"*Alors,*" Pierre said.

"I'll just open her up. Well, not that one." Owen got another. "Here we go." Owen uncorked the wine with great effort and gently decanted it over a candle flame while saying, "Maybe you and me could get some kind of deal going. I mean, I didn't just fall off the turnip truck. Who's going to take a red wine serious if it comes from Nebraska? We aren't especially known for our viticulture here, and you have to go clear to Omaha to find a good oenologist. But if you were to put *your* name on the label or just represented it some way, you could get my lovely darlings the admiration I personally think they deserve." Owen handed him a half-filled, red plastic cup. "At least those are my main bullet points. You can take the agenda any way you want from here."

Pierre suspiciously assessed the aroma of the purplish wine. "*Ce n'est pas du vin, c'est du sarcasme.*" (This isn't wine, it's sarcasm.)

"Don't judge that pretty miss too quick now. You gotta give the shy ones a second or two to introduce themselves."

Pierre sniffed again. "*C'est charmant. D'une manière brouillonne.*" (Charming. In a slovenly way.)

Owen assumed praise. "You don't know how it pleases me to hear you say that. All my friends think my reds are real tasty, but you, you've got a highly trained palate and an Old World discrimination that's woefully lacking in these climes."

Hopelessly, Pierre drank as if to debase himself, as if he were quaffing Sterno. He was prepared to wince, and his hand shot to his mouth as he forced a swallow, but then he just stared ahead, wide-eyed and mystified, for the finish of the wine was excellent, wholly unlike the poison he'd expected. "She has changed clothes!" he said.

"Oh, much better than that," Owen said, smiling. "She's shucked them off, and she is sheer beauty."

"*Mais oui,*" he said, "it's so!"

Owen swished the wine from side to side in his mouth

with a milk churning sound and then let it ooze down his throat. "A hint of cherries and green cigar in this one, isn't there?"

"*Il y a quelque chose.*" (There *is* something.)

"The secret's the water. All my grapevines are fed from Frenchman's Creek. We got our own little microclimate along those ruddy banks."

Pierre sipped again, evaluated, and offered flatly, "*C'est bon.*" (It's good.)

"Music to my ears," Owen said.

After finishing his plastic cup, Pierre handed it to Owen for more.

Owen got down another bottle of Big Red and grinned as he examined its vintage. "We beat Florida State in the Orange Bowl this year."

8

At four o'clock, Carlo Bacon locked the front door to
the Main Street Café, put on his kitchen oven mitts, and
hauled out of the Chefmaster oven a tray of lamb spring
rolls that he'd later dress with mango chutney. On a butcher
block table was a yellow King's Ransom rose with a handwritten tag that read "To the fairest." Clenching the rose in
his teeth, he took off his "Kiss the Cook" apron, went out
the kitchen's screen door with his tray of hors d'oeuvres,
and headed toward his garage apartment behind Mrs.
Christiansen's rooming house.

Against the tool bench wall of the garage was a freezer a

sizeable Angus could ruminate in. Humming "You Saved the Best for Last" he wrapped the tray of spring rolls in cellophane and nestled them inside the freezer next to a tray of wild mushroom risotto cakes and frosted containers of crab cakes and scallops enclosed in bacon. Waiting for his free time tomorrow was the four-tiered wedding cake of marzipan and chocolate ganache. The field greens with Cockburn pears and the main course of lobster and filet mignon he would have to prepare on the morning of the ceremony.

Carlo trudged up the garage stairs to a grandmotherly apartment furnitured in Mrs. Christiansen's hand-me-downs, and immediately dialed Dick Tupper's phone number. "Dick?" he said. "Carlo. What're you doing?"

"Getting into character," Dick said.

"Well, I've got a trade-last for ya."

Dick was a trifle slow on the uptake.

"You have to trade me some good gossip first."

"Oh, yeah. Um, Orville told me your coffee's just about as fresh and tasty as anything out there."

Carlo sighed. "It's the water."

"Well, I'm not very good at this," Dick said.

"Hokay," Carlo said. "Your trade-last is a certain mademoiselle is mighty interested in you."

There was a pause while the cattleman suppressed his

glory and delight, and then Dick frugally conceded, "She seems real nice."

"Maybe you should reciprocate."

"Oh jeez."

"How's this? I'll buy a yellow rose and say it's from you."

"All right," Dick allowed. "My sis always liked that brand called Summer Sunshine."

"I'm thinking King's Ransom. More fragrant."

"Or an Eclipse would be good."

"King's Ransom it is then."

"Appreciate it, Carl."

"Old habits die hard, don't they."

"Carl-*o*," Dick said.

Hanging up the phone, Carlo fell back onto his green chintz sofa and pulled his scrawled-in wedding planner into his narrow lap. So much yet to do, and she'd given him no clue about the invitations. With the weight and texture of the paper stock he felt confident, but although he'd slyly offered Iona plenty of post–lunch hour chances to indicate a favorite font in his printer's guide, she'd only regarded his inquiries strangely, as if Bodoni were interchangeable with Palantino or Fairfield italic. All he had was the wording. "The honour of your presence is requested in the marriage

of Miss Iona Christiansen to Carlo Bacon, Saturday, the
_____ of _____."

To be filled in later.

The affair itself would be al fresco, around noontime
and under the shingle oak shade trees beside Saint Bernard's
Church over there on Third Street, the Reverend Picarazzi
officiating. Chantilly lace gowns, layered organza, or tiers
of tulle with little pearl beading. And for him a stroller or
morning coat, with striped pants and a four-in-hand tie.

The hitch in his scheme was that Iona had no clue of it
and she really ought to be involved—or so his *Modern Bride*
hinted. And then there was the problem of the newly avail-
able Dick Tupper. She'd been trying to hide it since high
school, but Iona was crazily in love with him, had been
goofy about the older man since she was a little girl, even
high-tailed it to Omaha because she thought she'd do injury
to his wife over how she was mistreating him. So it was for-
tunate, Carlo thought, that Natalie and Pierre so glam-
orously waltzed into town. The mademoiselle was the kind
of independent, educated, put-together lady Dick would be
enchanted by, and Pierre, he was sure, was one of those
wealthy, suave, and handsome louts that even smart women
went ga-ga over. Carlo felt sure he need only play the
spaniel, the pert and nimble spirit of mirth, and when Dick's

attentions were wildly misdirected, and Iona's foolish choice became crushingly clear, Carlo would be there to commiserate, to superpraise her parts, to hold Iona as she cried, to offer forgeries of grief and insult, to agree that men were heels, lechers, scoundrels, and skunks—but not you, Carlo, you're different, Carlo, you're so generous, gentle, and good.

The liquor of such thoughts intoxicated him and it would be six before Carlo got into his Revels costume as the Marquis de Sade.

In Owen's living room, fourteen opened bottles of mixed shapes and sizes stood upright on the red carpet and, affected by drink, Pierre crawled on his hands and knees from one to another, sniffing inside with his scholarly nose as Owen talked on the telephone. "Orville? Owen here. Say, that wine-tasting day after tomorrow? Don't ask me how, but I came up with a genuine French *négociant* to be there. . . . *Négociant*. . . . A merchant. . . . Means he sells wines. . . . Uh huh. All the way from Paris. . . . No, not Texas; France. . . . On a bus. . . . Well, I s'pose he *flew* across the ocean. . . . A *lot* of people do. . . . You ask him that on Friday. And get the word out. . . . Okay. *Au revoir*." Owen hung up the phone. "Low-brow. Works on a snowplow in winter."

Pierre slunk against an ottoman, thinking. "Are these use-ed bottles?"

Owen nodded. "I get 'em for a nickel a piece from the café and the Last Chance Saloon over there in Three Pillows."

"The bouquet that I first thought so strange, he comes from the bottles, not the Big Red. You must sterilize."

"Forewarned is forearmed," Owen said.

"And always, always the Bordeaux bottles; never the Cutty Sark; never the Aunt Jemima."

"I'll jot it on my shirt cuff," Owen said, and hunkered next to Pierre, his elbows on his knees. "This is what I've been missing. The give and take. The badinage. The happy workshop atmosphere where strong opinions are meted out, not in a spirit of jealousy, but in a transparent desire to improve the final product."

Pierre was at a loss.

Owen was brimming with a notion, but was holding on and tamping it down for fear it would burst out as an abject plea. But finally he could resist no more and said with the quietness of the sober-minded, "The fact is, we could go halvesies on it."

"Have-sees?"

Owen stood and silently paced, his hand to his chin, prowling and ruminating, then turned and sat against the dining room sideboard with Husker dishware in it. He waved a hand at his surroundings. "House I grew up in. The gas station? My dad's. And here I am, in my thirties, big-boned, no wife or kids, just a fool of a Husker fan with a job any child could do and one great big impossible dream. You can make that dream come true, *mon frère*." Owen's head hung. "Hell, I feel like I'm proposing here. Am I coming on too strong?"

Pierre answered weakly, "We are hardly even friends."

Owen punched his left palm with his fist. "I *knew* it! I always *rush*! I'm such an *idiot*!" With frustration and shame, he stomped his shoes alternately, shaking the house. Owen faced him bleakly. "So where do we go from here?"

In the gas station office a frail female voice trilled, "Yoo hoo!"

Owen shot up and walked towards it. "Aunt Opal?" he called.

When Owen opened the office door, Pierre heard the elderly woman say in a faint giggle, as if it were risqué, "We'd like to rent *Gigi* for tonight."

"Well, I aim to please," Owen said.

Pierre tipped a final inch of wine into his plastic cup and sipped it as the transaction was completed. And then Owen closed the privacy door behind him again, no doubt wondering if their friendship had been chilled by the cold demands of business. But Pierre held up a bottle in the shape of a hula dancer and waggled its empty hips. "We have finished the one-point loss to Kansas State."

Owen lifted up another bottle from the floor, read its back label, and woefully announced, "Miami."

"*Encore!*" Pierre said, and held out his plastic wine cup.

The kitchen screen door creaked open and Dick Tupper made a grand entrance, his mustache waxed, his manner lacquered, costumed as he was in the scarlet satin cloak, soutane, and biretta of Cardinal de Richelieu. He held out a frock coat, tights, patent leather pumps, and a Louis XIV powdered white wig as he said, "I got your getup here, Pierre."

And so The Revels were royally begun at the fairgrounds that evening, the citizens of Seldom milling about like *Les Misérables* in the costumes of French chambermaids, urchins, revolutionaries, streetwalkers, and Parisian apaches, with one lone Mahatma Gandhi unsure of his history.

Mademoiselle Clairvaux wore a powdered white turban of a wig and an ornate Marie Antoinette dress whose architecture pinched her waist like an hourglass and made her still-youthful chest resemble melons riding on a shelf. She was given the job of cutting the ribbon at the weedy entrance to the carnival rides, and of announcing onstage what image a horrible mime was trying to convey: "Here he is trapped inside a box. See? He is feeling the many sides with his hands." "And now a wind is blowing him. We see it is very strong. Oh, he's lost his hat."

And then Pierre was forced to go up on stage in his silly leotards, crushed velvet pantaloons, and wig of a thousand ringlets, acting the part of the Sun King and shouting out the faulty French on a scroll that intended to detail how Bernard LeBoeuf chanced upon the area while trapping mink and thought he'd seldom encountered such pretty country. Owen shot a cannon into a cornfield as soon as Pierre concluded, and the wildly applauding Seldomites heaved their *bonnets rouges* high into the air, shouted a mysterious phrase they seemed to think was French, and then immediately commenced their Kiss-a-Pig Contest. (Won again by Chester Hartley, an old bachelor who raised barrows and gilts on a farm just east of Three Pillows.)

As king of The Revels Pierre was called upon to fire the starter's pistol that initiated the demolition derby, and he watched in stunned wonder as twelve cars peeled out in reverse, swerving to crash tail-first into each other, their trunk lids flying up and nodding, their mufflers and chassis scouring the earth, their wadded fenders floundering uselessly, until only Bert Slaughterbeck's new Buick was still running and he squirmed out the driver's side window and held his arms high in victory before he looked at his wrecked and steaming car somewhat quizzically, as if the consequences of the competition were something he had not completely thought through.

Meanwhile Natalie threw the switch that electrified the carnival's lighting, which was yellow in order to discourage a hundred varieties of whining insect, and she delivered queenly waves to the shrieking children on rides that were called the Zipper, the Tilt-a-Whirl, the Upsy-Daisy, the Scared Rabbit. She was then permitted to go back to Mrs. Christiansen's rooming house, where she changed into a white sundress and affectionately sniffed her yellow King's Ransom rose as she watched with interest the video of *Gigi* with Marvyl and Owen's Aunt Opal.

A house north and across the street, Dick joined Owen and Pierre for chicken wings and Falstaff beer and their viewing of Marlon Brando, Karl Malden, Ben Johnson, and Owen's friend Slim Pickens in a Western called *One-Eyed Jacks*. The Sun King had shed his wig, Cardinal Richelieu his scarlet biretta, and Owen found the good manners to hide the bulge of his codpiece with his untucked peasant shirt, but otherwise the three were still in their hose and regalia, which gave their viewing of the Western a certain incongruity. Pierre slumped on the sofa with jet lag, but he had never seen the movie and found himself riveted. Owen was less so. He asked, "You sure you wouldn't rather catch *Hobson's Choice*? Or *Witness for the Prosecution*? I'm in a Charles Laughton mood tonight."

No one answered him.

"*Ruggles of Red Gap* then," Owen said. "Winsome comedy where Laughton is delightful as an English butler won in a poker game."

Still no answer.

"Elvis then. *Harum Scarum*? *The Trouble with Girls*?"

On the screen, an outlaw played by Ben Johnson taunted the outlaw played by Marlon Brando in a saloon poker game, saying, "How about some of your cash there, Romeo?"

Owen finished a chicken wing and tossed it into a rapidly filling Husker wastebasket. Still unsatisfied, he got another, defeated it with just a few chews, and grinned with red barbeque sauce on his lips. "Hey, this chicken tastes just like frog," he joked.

Cardinal Richelieu cautioned, "Are you remembering your houseguest?"

Owen was shocked at his own rudeness. "No insult intended, Pete."

Pierre stared in uninsulted puzzlement, then returned to the movie. Ben Johnson was saying, "Well, maybe the boy's all petered out from playin' on the beach with that little jumpin' bean."

Owen got on his belly to find a tipped-over beer bottle underneath his La-Z-Boy, and in *One-Eyed Jacks* an outraged Marlon Brando jolted up from the poker table, yelling, "Get up, you scum-sucking pig!"

Dick said, "Talking to you, Owen."

Owen took a final gloomy swig from the beer he found as Brando upset the saloon's poker table with a crash. Owen was horrified. "We're outta beer, boys."

Neither Dick nor Pierre made a move, such things being beneath their station. Owen struggled his heft up. "Don't move a muscle," he told the friends who hadn't. "I'm the host. I'll go get more." And then he executed an Elvis move in his wide-bodied way, holding the Falstaff bottle as if it were a mike as he exited to the kitchen. "Thank ya'll ver' much, thank ya." And then he went outside, yelling, "Owen has left the building!"

Watching Pierre in an assaying way, Dick straightened his prelate's soutane at his thighs and crossed his red-stockinged ankles. "You been enjoying your trip through America's spacious skies and amber waves of grain?"

Pierre regally answered, "No."

"Seems to me I'd be pretty happy traipsing just about anywhere with such a pleasant companion."

Pierre shrugged. "Perhaps, but only if he lets *me* pick out ze wines."

"Wasn't talking about Owen," said Dick. "I was talking about Mademoiselle Clairvaux."

"Oh," Pierre said. "Her."

They watched *One-Eyed Jacks*. Brando was saying, "You got right on the edge. You mention her once more and I'm gonna tear your arms out."

Dick asked, "You two on the permanent outs?"

"What does it means, this 'outs'?"

"In other words, you got a future together?"

Pierre fell into a crotchety mood, as was his wont. "She is my *past*," he said. His fingers made antlers beside his head and he fluttered them wildly. "She is the craziness in my brains. She is so frus-*trat*ing and difficult and full of idiotic ideas."

"Well, maybe it's good you're taking a vacation from each other."

Owen sashayed back inside just then, cold beer cans weighting down the pockets of a blue Hawaiian shirt he'd changed into and on his skull a leafy headdress with Falstaff beer cans hung over each ear and plastic tubes feeding the liquid into his mouth when he sucked them. Owen grinned. *"Brew Hawaii!"*

Pierre arfed like a seal as Owen had instructed him to, and Owen tossed him a frosty one.

And Dick said, "I can see how Natalie must offend your delicate sensibilities."

10

Wednesday evening in Mrs. Christiansen's rooming house was serene. A hard-of-hearing old woman named Nell was sleeping in her Victorian room upstairs, as was Onetta, the mannish postmistress whose hobby was collecting the hundred varieties of barbed wire. Each of them claimed to be "plumb worn out" by The Revels. The sole teenaged girl in the house was a beautician named Ursula whose hair was, for the instant, orange and whose face was agleam with silver piercings, but she and her friends were out cruising the fairground's parking lot in an Econoline van. Iona was in the basement hooting "Hoo,

hoo" as she kicked and threw punches in accordance with the shouted instructions on her Tae Bo tape. And Natalie, Mrs. Christiansen, and Owen's Aunt Opal were sitting in a yellow-furnitured parlor while the video of *Gigi* played on the VCR. Mrs. Christiansen and Opal were humped over a card table and cooperating in putting together a puzzle of a basket of colorful yarns and puffy calico kittens. Natalie lounged on the yellow sofa in the frilly white sundress and she was offending the ladies by tucking her nude feet and calves sideways on the cushion so that the skin of her sunbrowned thigh was overmuch on exhibit. Opal sighed over the Continent's moral decline as she forced in a puzzle piece of kitten whiskers. She turned to Natalie and asked, "After you ditched your loverboy in such haste, how did you fritter away your afternoon?"

Natalie had never seen *Gigi* before and was caught up in the final chapters of the plot. Without turning, she flatly said, "We cooked dinner."

"And she did the dishes afterwards," Mrs. Christiansen said. "Without my beseeching, I might add."

Opal called to Natalie, "Have you noticed how nice your hands feel?"

Natalie frowned quizzically at her, then at her hands. They did feel softer, creamier, even childlike. "Yes!"

Opal was trying to wedge in a puzzle piece. "We feel like that all the time here. The healing properties of Frenchman's Creek ought to be a science project. Of course, it isn't exactly Lourdes, but we aren't so high and mighty as you people over there in Europe." She fiercely pounded a puzzle piece and the card table jumped.

Mrs. Christiansen cautioned, "Opal! Would you try to be friendly to one of our houseguests for once?"

"I just won't speak then," Opal said, and she made a zipper motion over her lips. She blankly stared at the television. Heading into the final triumphant scene of *Gigi*, Hermione Gingold said, "Thank Heaven . . ."

And Maurice Chevalier fell into song: ". . . for little girls."

Opal listened to the song for a minute, a silence which seemed to her almost impolitely protracted. She could go no longer without talking. "Oh, if a man would just once croon to me like he does."

Mrs. Christiansen said, "We hope in vain, Opal."

"Are you having a hard time following this picture show?"

"I haven't been paying attention."

She called, "Natalie, what's happening in the picture show?"

Natalie was heading into the kitchen for a soda. "*Elle va se marier*," she said.

Mrs. Christiansen translated, "She's getting married."

"Oh, so that's why she's here!" Opal said.

Mrs. Christiansen glanced up in puzzlement. "Who?"

Opal pointed to the kitchen. "She is. She's getting married here."

Mrs. Christiansen said, "I had no idea!"

"Well, looks like I'm one up on *you* for once."

Mrs. Christiansen considered the situation. "Why *here*, do you suppose?" And when Natalie walked back in with a waterglass fizzing with Coca-Cola, Marvyl asked, "*Pourquoi êtes-vous venue ici?*" (Why did you come here?)

Natalie indifferently said, "Pierre," and fell back onto the sofa.

Opal hissed discreetly, "She said Pierre chose us." She placidly held up an ill-fitting puzzle piece and trimmed a third of it with her scissors.

Mrs. Christiansen turned to Natalie. "Have you thought about your shower, dear?"

"*Pardon, Madame?*"

"Won't you have it here?"

She began to doubt her freshness. "If you like."

Opal asked in a hushed tone, "Question her as to when this wedding is supposed to take place."

Mrs. Christiansen asked, "Was it to be this weekend, Natalie?"

"Excuse me?"

Opal said, "*I* could have asked in English. I thought you were going to speak French."

Mrs. Christiansen flapped a hand disdainfully at Opal and continued, "You and Pierre. This weekend?"

Natalie was surprised she knew about their deadline, but uncertainly nodded. "*Oui, Madame.* Saturday. Noon."

"Oh, I'm so *excited*," Mrs. Christiansen said. "I haven't known you but a few hours and I already think of you as family."

Natalie watched in mystery as Mrs. Christiansen went upstairs.

Gigi ended and the videoplayer chirred into Rewind.

With fists squishing her cheeks and her elbows propped on the card table, Opal judged the wrecked puzzle. The left kitten looked like a handsickle now, and its playmate, she was forced to admit, was distinctly ogreish. She skeptically considered Natalie. "You play checkers, missy?"

Natalie shook her head. A soft breeze billowed the window curtains and she noticed the fragrance of clean air and watered lawns like a long-sought invitation quietly slipped under a door. "*Il fait beau*," she said, meaning the weather was fine, and she got up from the sofa and walked outside as Opal squinnied her cautious eyes with suspicion.

She strolled into a stately night that was silent but for a few crickets and the hints of music and excited children at the fairgrounds a half-mile away. She could see noiseless semis on the highway, the house and yard lights of a far-off farm, the haze of the Milky Way in a vast society of stars. And then she heard the truck door slam shut at Owen's gas station and she held a hand in front of her face as its headlights turned on.

Opal was tilted half out of her chair to watch Natalie when Iona came up from the basement in her tight one-piece workout suit, the Tae Bo tape in her hand. Immediately Opal got into an upright sitting position and shifted her focus to a stern perusal of Iona's scanty and revealing outfit. She said, "You girls today seem intent on giving mankind anatomy lessons."

"You told me that yesterday, too."

"Well, it bore repeating."

Iona patted her face with a towel as she looked into the kitchen. "Where'd Natalie go?"

Opal pretended to wedge in a puzzle piece. "She said something in French about her beau. That's a boyfriend, right? She probably just had to see him."

Iona went to the screened front door and saw a red pickup truck idling in the middle of Main Street, its headlights on, and

Dick Tupper happily leaning out his truck window to simper and chat with Natalie. She was giggling. Worried and in shock, Iona looked to Opal. "Are they *together*?"

Opal got out her scissors again and feigned disinterest by refusing to take a gander outside. "Well, of course they are," she said.

"How'd they meet?"

"Who knows? Maybe through one of those newspaper pages where girls with no sense say come and get it."

Iona hopelessly gazed out the front door again, a hand pressing her towel to her mouth as she watched. She sagged a little when she saw Natalie's fingers lightly graze the truck's chrome door handle. She said, "I have had a crush on him for so long. Ever since I was a little girl."

She'd lost Opal on that turn. "On *him*?" she asked. "That's impossible!"

Iona sighed. "I know it is. But you can dream."

Owen and Pierre lurched out of the gas station bungalow with Falstaffs in every hand and failed to notice Natalie as they tilted against each other and howled in an imitation of Elvis in *Blue Hawaii*, "Take . . . *my* . . . hand! Take my . . . whole . . . life . . . too! For I . . . can't . . . *help* . . . falling in *love* . . . with . . . you!"

Meanwhile, Mrs. Christiansen was hurrying down from

upstairs with a glamorous white Empire dress hanging over both arms. She gushed from the landing, "Won't she look gorgeous in this?"

Opal frantically waved her hands. She made hushing gestures. She pretended to cut her throat with her thumb.

Iona turned to Mrs. Christiansen. "Who will? When?"

Mrs. Christiansen thought. "Onetta. She so rarely wears dresses."

And Opal lamely said, "When she goes to the hardware store."

11

Sunrise in the Main Street Café. Wearing a spare pink waitress dress, Natalie helped Iona serve coffee and farmer's breakfasts to a crowd of thirty or more fulminating men. She'd found a pair of squarish, dark-framed eyeglasses that made her resemble the singer Nana Mouskouri, so the farmers and truckers were mostly at bay, but still she was a little overwhelmed by the shocking noise of yelled jokes, banging mugs, clacking plates, and the hollered chat of morning larks in overalls who all seemed hard of hearing. Plus, a way-turned-up radio voice was giving farm commodities prices from the Chicago Mercantile Exchange.

She was surprised by a tip left behind, but folded it into her apron pocket and withdrew with an empty coffeepot to the four-beaker coffee machine behind the counter. The din and commotion had quelled some and Iona took the opportunity for a respite, leaning on the pink Formica countertop and sipping a café au lait as she inspected the various species of maleness in the room. When Natalie rested on her elbows beside her, Iona said, "Look at my choices. Micah's gotten hitched about twice too often. Orville's homely and married. And Carlo Bacon is not exactly the sensible image of the Infinite."

Natalie was taken aback.

"Quote I learned in junior college," Iona said flatly. She considered a counter stool. "The Reverend's handsome, but he's a whatayacallit?"

"*Un célibataire?*"

"Right, a celebrate." She sipped some more coffee and panned the room. "Too old. Too fat. Just a kid. Way too ugly. Way too stuck on himself. Blah. Another blah. And him? Maybe if I get drunk enough." She sighed. "My town, Natalie. Party, party."

The dull radio voice was saying, "Corn futures down a quarter. Wheat staying even. Soybeans falling fifteen cents . . ." as Owen and Pierre grandly entered.

"*Bonjour mes amis!*" Owen shouted.

Hearty greetings were exchanged, hands roughly shaken, guffaws forced, and Pierre eyed Natalie in a plum happy way, for he felt spruce and superior in his borrowed motorcycle boots and green mechanic's coveralls with the name "Harvey" stitched over the pocket. When he noticed Natalie's forbidding eyeglasses, he gleamed momentarily, then glanced away.

Owen said to Cecil, "*Permettez-moi de vous presenter Monsieur Pierre Smith.*"

Onlookers were stunned. Cecil asked, "What the hell was that?"

Owen answered, "I could *not* tell ya. Said it nice though, didn't I?" Owen slid into a booth and Pierre imitated him just as a good boy might his father. And then Dick nonchalantly sashayed in and the male greeting ritual was repeated until he slid into the booth next to Pierre.

Iona watched her rival watch Dick's entrance and then she watched the booth as Natalie went over with a handful of hooked cups and a round glass beaker of fresh coffee. Owen and Dick smiled up at the French waitress and seemed to exchange pleasantries, but Pierre stared at the salt and pepper shakers as if they would soon be his food. And Iona found herself transfixed by Pierre, for in those workman's clothes the Frenchman did not seem so rich and conceited as he first did to Iona, but like the wrongfully accused fugitive from the jailhouse who in dreams stole into her room at night and smelled of motor oil and sweat as he reclined on the mattress beside her and held his hand to her mouth and whispered, "Don't scream," as the sheriff searched the house in vain. And Dick Tupper was the opposite, no outlaw in him, no shame in his past, but upright, respectable, widely admired, a man who would not squander a fortune, lose his head, or fall in love with the little girl who carried Mason jars of lemonade to him way back when he was still married and the September harvest was hot.

She watched Natalie Clairvaux walk into the kitchen.

Carlo hastily hid a *Modern Bride* magazine under some dish towels and took the breakfast orders Natalie handed him. While perusing them, he said in a nonchalant way, "Quick as weeds are Cupid's arrows."

She stalled. "*Pardon?*"

Carlo swashed corn oil across the griddle with a housepainting brush as he said, "Tender feelings. Infatuation. Some call it love." The oil sizzled and popped until he poured a ladle of blueberry pancake mix. "We are sooner led by our hearts than our heads."

"Who?"

His Dick Tracy mustache rocked up on one side in his smirk. "Oh, no one. Empty speculation. And it could be he just wants to make you jealous."

"Pierre?"

"So you've noticed."

She felt she was being toyed with. "Food for thought," she said and went out to the dining room, wiping an ice water ring from the Formica counter as she watched a shy and smiling Iona return from Owen's boisterous booth.

Iona instantly told her, as if she were hiding a secret, "They needed cream," and then she hurried past Natalie into the kitchen.

Carlo grinned so widely at Iona it seemed insanity was just minutes away.

"Well, I made contact," she said.

Even as his foot began tapping, Carlo tried to act blithe by flipping a blueberry pancake with his spatula. "Was it like I told you?"

"Well, not really. Dick was a perfect gentleman, and Owen was Owen, but the French guy never said a peep."

Carlo seemed to ponder that as he flipped another pancake. "And weren't you just a little more interested in why he wasn't noticing you?"

She gave it some thought. "I guess."

"Well, there you go then. The French practically invented seduction; and you, my pretty one, are being seduced."

"Huh," Iona said.

Carlo tried to still his jittery leg by holding it firmly against the oven door, but it just made a thumping noise like a happy spaniel's tail. Iona gave him an inquisitive look. "Tell you what," he said. "We'll go out together for fun in the sun. You and me and Owen and him. See if he doesn't scope you out."

She was fixing her hair in a toaster's reflection. "Well, jeez," she said. "He's male, isn't he?"

But Carlo was lost in a prurient stare, confirming her assumptions.

Natalie was wringing out a hand towel in the sink as Iona exited from the kitchen and halted to lean casually on the Formica counter and stare across the dining room. She heard Iona say, "You got yourself a catch, girl." And though Iona meant Dick Tupper, Natalie presumed she meant Pierre, and she found herself watching her fiancé with other eyes until he and Dick and Owen finally left the café. She was hurt that Pierre ignored her.

12

At noon on Thursday Mrs. Christiansen took Natalie to the fairgrounds. Wearied from the first night of The Revels, Marvyl sportily hummed along beside her on a motorized sort of tricycle as Natalie meandered through the crowds past the various outdoor booths of The Revels: a French Foreign Legion shooting gallery with Algerian rifles and tin camels for targets; a miniature Eiffel Tower ring toss booth; a place where you could dunk a quite dry musketeer in a cow watering tank if you pitched a softball into a tin target with impossible speed and accuracy. Girlish screaming was issuing from a gloomy Bastille that was stocked full of hallways that headed nowhere, scarecrows and mannequins that hurled themselves at trespassers, and funhouse mirrors that so horribly misshaped a person that she might think unwillingly of the buttocks on her Aunt Dolly.

Natalie lagged behind to gaze at the "Weird Animals" exhibit where there was a pet spider monkey and a sign that read: "Howdy! My name is Stinky! I will clap my hands if you show me food!" And there was a thoroughly ordinary Afghan dog, quivering with embarrassment in a beret and a striped French sailor's suit. A marmalade cat with a Captain Video helmet was trapped inside a space suit made from aluminum foil. The owner was holding its front paws in the air, so the cat stood on its hind legs, its tail lashing. Zapping noises were piped in as ray guns feebly strafed the air. The sign around the cat's neck read: MARTIAN.

Mrs. Christiansen shoved her tricycle in reverse and swerved snakily back, a horn beeping, until Natalie caught up again. Mrs. Christiansen said, "The ladies were so pleased when they heard a cordon bleu from Paris was here to judge their cooking."

Natalie cautioned, "Madame, I am not a chef."

But Marvyl wasn't listening. "Carl Bacon did it once," she said, "but he's a tad persnickety. Last year we settled on a fry cook from Ogallala whose Oldsmobile was being fixed." She turned the tricycle toward a tent and motored inside. At once there were high-pitched cheers and thunderous applause from the many women at folding tables on which a wild assortment of foods were arrayed. Mrs. Christiansen stood up from her vehicle and put a finger to her lips in a teacherly way. Women quieted. "I have the honor of presenting to you the Queen of the Revels, Mademoiselle Natalie Clairvaux," she said. "Our guest taster. Now remember, she'll be judging both flavor and presentation. And you're not allowed to tell her what she's eating."

There were a few faint groans and protests.

Mrs. Christiansen shushed them with a hand and formally turned. "Natalie?"

Natalie walked uncertainly toward the first table of pies and pastries. She lifted a smidgen of lemon meringue pie with a plastic fork, put it in her mouth, and evaluated it. "*Très bien*," she said.

She shifted sideways and tilted forward to taste a Boston cream pie. She was getting into it, becoming a regular Julia Child. "*Intéressant*," she said, "*mais . . . agressif.*"

"Was it good?" the cook asked Mrs. Christiansen.

She got a pat of condolence on the forearm as they went on.

Lois Tetlow, a full-figured gal, was spilling out of a skimpy French maid's outfit as she presented a tray of muffins.

Mrs. Christiansen chided, "Lois!"

"Well, last year the judge was a man," Lois said.

Natalie nibbled some muffin and grew concerned. "Are they raisins?"

"Blueberries," Lois said, "but they mighta turned."

Natalie shifted over to Owen's Aunt Opal, who was humble to the point of unctuousness as she held up a faintly green rhubarb pie. Natalie hesitated with the dab on her fork. She took a full breath and tried the pie. She could not hide a wince.

Opal explained, "What's the point of a food competition if you don't get to experiment and be creative?"

Natalie was still masticating while seeking a place to spit.

Opal told Marvyl, "It just occurred to me that a little chili powder and Worcestershire sauce might put a sleepy old pie up on its hind legs."

"I'm sure it's unique," Mrs. Christiansen said, and then she looked ahead. "Oh no. Mrs. Zebrun made her Candied Tree Bark Surprise."

13

Natalie avoided food poisoning and rewarded herself with an afternoon nap at Mrs. Christiansen's rooming house. She woke at three to the sounds of cooking in the kitchen and took it upon herself to help out, cracking farm eggs into a great big bowl of cake mix as Opal and Mrs. Christiansen chopped and washed vegetables. Mrs. Christiansen announced, "We'll have a Waldorf salad first off on Saturday."

"Oh, I like that idea," Opal said.

"And then I thought a Châteaubriand would be nice for the main course."

"Uh huh. Kind of make her feel more at home."

"With onions and carrots *à brun*."

"You know what I think I'd like to try, Marvyl? Potatoes Lyonnaise."

Mrs. Christiansen frowned. "From a freezer package or from scratch?"

"The grocery freezer."

Mrs. Christiansen smiled. "Aren't you a dear?"

Opal whispered, "You don't think she had her heart set on French fries?"

And Marvyl whispered, "She hasn't *planned* a thing."

"'Cause if she does, those frozen kind you get in cartons are just so quick and easy . . ."

Mrs. Christiansen asked Natalie, "*Voulez-vous des pommes frites?*" (Would you like fried potatoes?)

She dumped egg shells into the trash compactor and slammed it closed. "Whatever you wish," she said.

Mrs. Christiansen spun back to Opal. "She's got a great deal on her mind, if you get my meaning."

"Oh, I do."

All three heard a faint rapping on the front screen door and tilted out toward the hallway. Reverend Dante Picarazzi was on the front porch in his black clerics and white Roman collar, his blue Yankees baseball cap in one hand as he shaded his eyes with the other and peered in through the screen. "Afternoon," he offered.

Opal jumped to the conclusion that he was there for her, though it would have been without precedent. She held a hand with a paring knife to her chest and said, "My word! It's the Reverend!"

Mrs. Christiansen smiled in a tut-tut way and said with innuendo, "Dante needs to iron out details with Mademoiselle Clairvaux."

Slowly the meaning dawned upon Opal. "Oh, I see. Oh yes, they really *have* to talk."

"Details?" Natalie asked.

Mrs. Christiansen looked to the front porch and called, "Wait there, Reverend. She'll be right out."

"Surely you could bend the house rules for a priest," Opal said.

And Mrs. Christiansen haughtily said, "That would be breaking the rules, not bending them."

Worriedly, Natalie went out to the front porch, full of mystery about the priest's visit, and found him swinging his legs like a kid on the glider that hung from the porch ceiling. His Yankees cap was jauntily cocked on his head, his running shoes dangled off the floor, and he was petting a mustache that was still twisted and waxed. With his characteristic torrent of words, the priest said, "Played Toulouse-Lautrec at The Revels. Nailed it." The Reverend patted a space beside him and as Natalie sat, he rushed on, saying, "I heard the whole megillah from Marvyl."

And Natalie, whose English, she'd thought, was good, had trouble with his Brooklynese and understood only "heard" and "from Marvyl."

"Sorry about the royal snafu. *Mea culpa*. Snail-mail you sent me? Tipping me off? Like a knucklehead I musta lost it."

She understood "Sorry," "snail," "lost."

"Oy, my desk," he said. He lifted a hand as high as his ear. "Stacked to here with bubkes."

With an excess of politeness she said, "I have never heard anyone speak so fast."

"Well that's me." The priest raised his right knee to tie a running shoe that must have been bought in the boy's department. She wondered if others also had the urge to tousle his hair. "Informed His Eminence about the glitch. Hemmed and hawed, but he's a mensch; plus he owed me. We got it locked in for Saturday. You cool with that?"

She watched him staring at her and she construed he'd asked a question that required an answer. She nodded her head.

"Right. You shlep up the aisle, deliriously happy, blushing right and left. I greet you and I do the booga-booga. We endure with smiles the fumbling for rings. I say this, I say that; you parrot it back. You know the routine. We need a rehearsal?"

She'd understood hardly a word. She shook her head no.

"Hiya, Dick," he said.

She glanced out to the front yard and saw Dick diffidently standing on the sidewalk in his cattleman's hat and boots. Shy as a suitor. "Wondered if Mademoiselle Clairvaux would like to go on a horseback ride."

"Well, that seems highly irregular to me," Opal said from inside the house.

Natalie tilted and saw that Mrs. Christiansen and Owen's Aunt Opal were hunched at the front screen door, overhearing.

"Oh, Opal," Mrs. Christiansen said. "She'll enjoy it! And he's a perfect gentleman. Aren't you, Dick Tupper."

"Oh, yes, ma'am."

She turned to Natalie. "You go ahead, dear. We'll manage the cooking."

With irritation, Opal reminded the widow, "Many hands make light work."

Mrs. Christiansen softly flicked at her friend's wrist and said to Dick, "She'll be right out."

The Reverend jumped down from the glider. "You go change. I have to schmooze with the lucky guy."

She thought, *What is schmooze?* But she told him, "I have enjoyed talking with you."

And Dante was already skipping down the steps as he said, "Natch."

She went upstairs to get into bluejeans, sneakers, and a soft white shirt. When she came out the cattleman was beaming at the foot of the front porch stairs, and she blushed at his happiness.

"What'd the Reverend have to say?" Dick asked.

"I have no idea."

"He's a New Yorker," Dick said, as if much, in such a manner, was explained. Warily looking into the house, he confessed, "I get real skittish around Mrs. Christiansen. She puts me back into high school whenever I'm around her."

On cue Mrs. Christiansen called, "You be careful with her, Dick Tupper!"

And he was no more than fourteen years old when he called, "Yes, ma'am!"

14

*H*olding onto the horses' bridles, Dick escorted a saddled paint-colored mare and sorrel stallion from the cool darkness of his red stables and into the stark August sunshine. Natalie was standing up on the first white board of the paddock fence and was scanning his groomed and handsome ranch property with fascination. Dick just stared at Natalie's beauty until she turned.

"You can ride Ida and I'll ride Shep," he told her. "Shep's got strict opinions about things."

She smiled and hopped down to the earth and he helped her fit a sneaker into the saddle's iron stirrup.

"I'll just give you a little boost," he said, but his hand accidentally wound up on her fine behind and he blushed, just as she did. "Oops," he said, and smiled bashfully for a few seconds before he got serious again. "Don't let go of Ida's reins or she just might take ya shopping."

She hunted the irregular verb in her memory before saying, "I have *ridden* a horse before."

"Oh, I could tell. You have that equestrian poise."

They rode out into the countryside through high rustling foxtail weeds that almost reached the cinches. Angus cattle were tearing up hanks of grass and blandly chewing in the sunshine, and some were full enough to lie down on their bellies and ruminate and stare.

Dick glanced over his shoulder. "You about got the hang of that horse?"

"Yes. She is very ... *docile*."

"Placid too," he said. He considered the shifting herd. "You know what we call those cows?"

"Angus?"

"And here I took you for a greenhorn."

"I have read all about the West."

"I used to read about the Count of Monte Cristo. Joan of Arc was my heart-throb when I was a boy."

"Have you ever been to France?"

"My dad was. 1944. Summertime."

She was pleased by the coincidence. "My mother, she is from Bayeux, in Normandy. We have visited Omaha Beach many times. My grandmother owns a hotel in Port-en-Bessin. On the shore of the English Channel."

"What was her first name?"

"Sophie."

"Don't recall him mentioning a Sophie. But then my dad had his head ducked too much to see a whole lot of the population. Did say your people were real cultured and friendly and happy to see him. He always appreciated that. S'pose your mother wasn't even born then."

"No."

"I wasn't either." He stared at her seriously. "In case you're wondering, I'm fifty-two." She said nothing. "So I guess that'd make you half my age."

She smiled. "And so I am a 'trophy' for you?"

"Well, no; you're a pleasant companion."

The horses wove around cottonwood trees and through shaded green timothy grass and ferns as Dick guided them alongside Frenchman's Creek. Wild deer feeding on the sapling leaves that they could reach had created a flat browse line on the underside of some young box elders and Dick educated Natalie on it. "Whole terrain hereabouts used to have so much wildlife an Eastern fella once called it 'the paradise of hunters.'" Admiring it, he said, "Pretty country, isn't it?"

Natalie was enchanted. "Yes! Like a cigarette ad!"

"Well, I s'pose I would've compared it to Eden, but each to her own vista."

She told him she'd visited America the first time as a junior in high school. She was an exchange student and was sent to Cambridge, Massachusetts, as the guest of husband and wife mathematics professors and their two appalling children. She could not believe how boring their lives were. Clavichord music. Algebra problems at the dinner table. Wine only on holidays. And no television—

Dick interrupted, "No *television?* Sheese. Was there *plumbing?*"

"We are talking ten years ago. Rules may have changed."

"No television," he repeated.

Shep furiously shook his head and horseflies twined in the air.

"And they were strict vegetarians," Natalie said.

The cattleman reached out and touched her hand in consolation. "You poor child."

Which was not so bad, but neither the husband nor wife

could cook and seemed to subsist only on rice cakes and chunks of tofu.

Dick Tupper gritted his teeth. "The bastards!"

She continued. The household insisted on speaking their gruesome French whenever she was around and so she was forced to become their teacher and each grew to hate her corrections and she spent much of the nine months in the United States upstairs in her attic room, weeping with loneliness and filling thirteen journals with poetry and self-pity. And when she got back to France her teachers claimed she spoke better English *before* she went to America.

"Well, as far as that goes, your language skills may be ruint if you stay in Seldom too dang long."

They rode up a slope to a ridgetop of tan prairie that was surrounded by green patches of skunkbush and dog-wood, and then they went down a hillside steep as stairsteps as Dick named the green ash, basswood, and bur oak trees. Natalie pointed to green herbs in the shaded understory and asked, "What's that?"

And Dick told her, "Wood nettle."

"And this?" she asked.

"Wild columbine," he said. "Stops flowering in June." She shifted in the saddle to look down at a plant near her stir-rup and Dick immediately named it, "Jack-in-the-pulpit."

She smiled. "Are you a botanist?"

"Well, I've lived here all my life. You just naturally like to know who your neighbors are."

She faced forward. "Nature is not so interesting to Pierre."

Considerately, he said, "Oh, he's expert in other things, I imagine."

She seemed not to approve of those other things.

Willows colonized the floodplain of another part of Frenchman's Creek where the pebbled sand was hard-going for the horses, but at a turning they strode at a quicker pace toward a spot they seemed to remember. Shade trees and soft grasses moved in the breeze and creek water pillowed over smooth round stones near the bank. Dick jumped down from Shep and helped Natalie down from her horse. "Go ahead and give me your foot. I'll try not to get too personal with ya this time."

Natalie smiled. "I am not bothered."

Dick walked her down to the creek bank with a red picnic blanket that he flung out and let float on the air and softly settle. She sat on it while he squatted beside her, unscrewing a canteen filled with Owen's wine as he told her, "French trappers used to ship pelts from hereabouts to fur companies back east. One fella's name was Bernard

LeBoeuf. Had a rough time of it, I guess, and thought he was a goner. Wandered around like a zombie and fell into the water here. Woke up an hour later halfways healed. Had himself a new lease on life."

"What was his problem?"

Dick thought about it. "Thirst, for one thing." He paused. "And I guess a grizzly bear before that. Torn up pretty good. Ever since, this has been called Frenchman's Creek and tales of its magical powers are still being told."

"And do you believe these tales?"

"Why I brought ya down here."

She held out a plastic cup and he poured wine into it. "Is it you want to make love with me?"

He hesitated, and then got a plastic cup for himself and filled it. "Well now, I'm a tad bit old-fashioned about that."

"What is it you want then, Mister Tupper?"

Skiffs of sunshine rocked on the water as he watched it move. "I'll tell ya what I have. Twelve hundred acres plus farm buildings, machinery, and feeder pens. I have a four-bedroom Victorian house that's just had itself done over by an interior desecrator named Mitzi. I have five percent of the last Holiday Inn you passed on the highway, nine percent of the largest Chrysler Dodge and Plymouth dealership west of Lincoln, and half a dozen employees that call me

Mister Tupper. What I don't have is a wife." He paused. "She left me high and dry."

"She was stupid," Natalie said.

"Don't expect me to argue the matter." Dick looked sentimentally at her and then was ashamed of his forwardness. "Hell, I'm too old for the hunt anyway."

Natalie protested, "*Mais non!* You are not old!"

Dick recited, "'Cold are the hands of time that creep along relentlessly, destroying slowly but without pity that which yesterday was young. Alone our memories resist this disintegration and grow more lovely with the passing years.'" He smiled with some embarrassment. "I got that from a movie."

Natalie was nodding. "But yes! *The Palm Beach Story*. I like very much the films of Preston Sturges."

Dick considered her with amazement. "Wonder if we met in a past life."

She watched as some shade trees furiously shook. She could see a pair of shining minks playing and twirling in the creek, the noise of it shifting over the rocks with the sound of party conversation. She said, "No. This is my first life. That is why I'm so happy and surprised."

Dick took pleasure in that. "So you like it here."

"I *love* it here!" she said. "It is so odd and old-fashioned and naive, and no one is trying to be smart."

"Are you sure those are compliments?"

She put a hand to his cheek. "And you, Deek Tup-pair. You are as faithful and honest and natural as a horse."

Each of them looked to Shep as he nuzzled into shaded grass, his tail whisking right and left. But it soon turned into an unfortunate moment and they turned away.

"Horses'll do that," Dick said.

And then they heard a hollering, rollicking group of Owen, Carlo, Iona, and Pierre sailing down the creek on tractor tire inner tubes, squirting Owen's wine out of goatskins, the men shirtless and sunburnt and in jean cut-offs, Iona luscious in a leopard print string bikini and intently watching the man and woman in the shade as she floated past.

Carlo was giddy at finding the picnickers fulfilling his plot and with a squiggly smile tilted out on his inner tube to see Iona's face. She seemed properly disappointed as an eddy spun her away. Carlo gave Dick a puckish thumb's up.

Owen yelled, "Sybaritic pleasures, Dick!"

Dick yelled, "Don't make me wash your mouth out with soap!" And then he smiled and said to Natalie, "Having themselves a time."

Pierre swirled around in his inner tube in order to scowl at Natalie on the bank. She haughtily smiled at his jealousy, and then he found a swift passage of water and flew out of sight.

Still staring after him, she said, "Have you noticed how Monsieur Smith does not fit in here? He is like the fish out of water." She craned her neck to see farther down the creek.

"We better go," Dick said, and helped her up.

She faced her swain. "And then will you kiss me?"

He smiled. "Oh, I reckon I could do that much."

They kissed.

She liked it. And he did, too.

15

Children were squealing on rides at the Seldom fairgrounds and the night just above the horizon was brilliantly streaked with the scarlet and yellow and blue neon lights of wild machines and game arcades and food booths filled with pizza slices, hot dogs, and sweets. Waiting their turn at the Dairy Delite were Iona and Pierre, each wearing jean cutoffs under Owen's green gas station shirts. Pierre's hung loose but Iona's was tied above her firm-muscled stomach. She handed Pierre a vanilla ice cream cone that a churring machine had stacked like a minaret, and he sculpted it with his tongue as they strolled.

Iona asked, "When you got here? Why was Natalie upset with you?"

"We have an argument," he said.

"And what was the topic?"

Pierre shrugged and said, "She says I never pay attention to her . . . or something like that."

"Are you sure it wasn't about the wedding?"

Pierre halted a second in confusion, and then he resumed his stride.

"Don't worry," Iona said. "You don't have to pretend. Anyone can see you still like her. Otherwise you wouldn't be so mean."

She'd lost him. She seemed to want a comment. "But it's *you* I like," he said.

She cocked her head and became coy. "Why?"

Pierre stepped away to give her a hair-to-toe appraisal as he licked the balconies of the ice cream. Even in Owen's shirt she was gorgeous. "But you are so natural and beautiful!" he exclaimed. "Elemental. Passionate. *Erotique*. Like Brigitte Bardot before she went crazy for animals."

She blushed. "I'm not like that, really. I just want normal things. To be friendly to people. To love and be loved. To get to know someone really well and to have him know me in the same way." She paused. "You probably don't think that's very ambitious."

"But no! To love and be loved is the *highest* ambition!"

She smiled. "You're pretty good at this, aren't you."

"At what?"

"Romancing a girl."

Complacently, he said, "Well, I'm French." And then he continued his hobby, turning his shrinking ice cream cone this way and that. The soft August heat was melting it too fast and he was not practiced in the art of such eating. "*Il fait trop chaud pour une glace,*" he said. (It's too hot for ice cream.)

"Are you getting it all over your hand?"

"I fear yes."

"Here." She licked a tear of ice cream from the cone and then coquettishly licked some more from his hand.

"Sank you."

"Good flavor," Iona said.

"*Vraiment?*" (Truly?) He licked his cone and then Iona's hand. She giggled. "Yes," he said, "very good that way."

She saw people who knew her and all seemed to have children either on the rides or waiting for them. All stared at Iona with worship or leers or silent opinions, some of the men nodding in a hidden way or waving hello with the twitch of a finger. She told Pierre, "You don't know what it's like growing up here. With it being so claustrophobic. I mean, they're the salt of the earth, but every person in Seldom has known every blessed thing about me since I was one year old. You can't grow up, really, you can't change, you can't even get a little wild. You're in front of all these cameras. You aren't supposed to be perfect; you're just supposed to be predictable." She paused. "Why don't we get out of here?"

She took him by the hand and turned south, away from the booths and exhibits and toward a night where lightning bugs flickered and trembled and described strange golden alphabets in the air. A healthy scent of alfalfa drifted in from the fields. She got to a white plank fence and jumped her rump onto the top rail before quickly swinging her lithe legs over to the greensward on the other side. Pierre finished the remainder of his ice cream cone and wiped his hands on Owen's green shirt before holding onto a fence post as he struggled over the fence and bulkily fell onto the lawn. She helped him up and he saw they were on the sixteenth tee of the golf course. A 412 yard, par 4. Water hazard on the left. Tricky green. She slipped her right arm around his waist and he pulled her closer so that there was friction as they strolled.

"So who are you really?" she asked.

"Gérard Depardieu. But younger."

She laughed. "I need more."

"My grandfather was British. My grandmother, she was a countess. I have herited from her . . ."

"*In*herited."

". . . a little castle and—I am losing the English—*une vigne?*"

"Vineyard?"

"*C'est juste.* And from my father I have the job in the family firm, which is buying and selling the wines in all the world. I am the director of—"

"Your *job?*" She gazed at him in amazement. "That is *such* a male answer."

"I have left out what?"

"Emotions, for starters." And he seemed so mystified that she decided to prompt him. "Are you afraid of anything?"

"Spiders."

She could see he was withholding. "And that's all?"

"Another question please."

"Heights? Snakes? Failure? Kitchen appliances?"

"Kitchen appliances?"

She felt caught out. "But we were talking about you."

He stilled as he thought. "I have sree older brothers. All very good at business. And for them I am merely a . . . *jouisseur?*"

She considered the possibilities. "Playboy?"

"Exactly."

"*Are* you one?"

His head ducked in his French way as his mouth puffed a soft *puh* at the indisputable. "It is the role I have been assigned. I cannot do otherwise."

"And you're afraid of what?"

Squirming with uneasiness, he said, "Are not playboys always, finally . . . fools?"

"So you're afraid of making a fool of yourself," she said.

"I have said enough."

"And that's why you try to act so bristly and cold and highfalutin. So no one gets inside."

In an effort at deflection he asked, "Is it that you have studied the *psychologie?*"

She flatly stated, "I just listen to Doctor Laura on the radio. Oh, and hot tip, Pierre: Don't ever call in."

Soulfully gazing into her eyes, he said, "She could teach me about my heart's desire."

"Which is?"

Without smiling, he quoted her. "To love and be loved."

Iona smiled. "Clever boy."

"Really, Iona. I think it is so."

"Well, I'm touched."

"And you?" he asked. "Who are *you*, Iona?"

"The facts?"

"We begin there."

"I'm twenty-three years old. Raised in Seldom. My mom passed when I was a girl, and my dad was off in Timbuktu by then, so I've been halfways on my own for ages. Brownies, Girl Scouts, Four-H Club. Went to high school over in Three Pillows. I was a football cheerleader in the fall, a gymnast in winter, and played girl's softball in the spring. And I have a letter sweater to prove it. Mister Tupper coached us. Average student. I've had nine semi-cute boyfriends since puberty, and only three broken hearts. Oh, and I was queen of the Snowflake Frolic *and* the Senior Prom. Attended Metro Tech Community College, Associate of Arts degree, and then I got a job at Mutual of Omaha. Shared an apartment with three other girls. We quarreled all the time. Ran out of hot water every morning. Went into credit card debt, shopping just to soothe the melancholy, and decided Seldom wasn't so bad. I've been back with my grandma for three months now."

"Madame Christiansen. *Très gentille*."

"She is. I love her to pieces, but she thinks things ought

to be the way they were when she was a girl. She caught me with a guy in my Omaha apartment and she got so stricken! Like I was defiled." She paused. "I'm afraid of being a fallen woman. And my heart's desire is to fall for someone."

The sand bunkers that fronted the sixteenth green were half a wedge shot away. Pierre sought a sympathetic response. But he sought in vain. "It is never easy, is it," he said.

Iona noticed his vague detachment and said, "Here I am griping and doing the poor-me bit and tiring you out with the translating."

He admitted, "English is a difficult language for me. I have not the . . . *vocabulaire*. I feel *stupide*?"

"But you're not! I can tell. Which words were you hunting for?"

Pierre frowned with thoughtfulness and asked, "How does one say in English, 'You have beautiful breasts'?"

Iona blushed as she looked down at her shirt and said, "Exactly like that." After a pause, she said, "I'll bet it's prettier in French though."

Pierre haughtily said, "Of course." His hand went to her blonde hair. "The hairs . . . *les cheveux*." He floated both hands onto her face and she turned it against his right palm. "Your eyes so blue . . . *les yeux couleur d'azurs*." His right thumb lightly traced her lips as he whispered, "The mouth . . . *la bouche*." And his mouth neared hers as he said, "The kiss . . . *le baiser*." They kissed and she seemed to swoon a little. Pierre theatrically withdrew from her and settled onto the freshly mown fairway, and she got down on the fairway, too, lying half on top of him, one thigh beside his, her forearms propping her up off his chest, a hand toying with his wild mane of hair. A moon of pearl was shining down on them.

Iona asked, "How do you say you've got a crush on somebody?"

"A . . . crush?"

"Say you're romantic about someone you just met."

Pierre replied meaningfully, "*J'ai le béguin pour toi*."

She said as if just practicing it, "*J'ai le béguin pour toi*." She smiled shyly. "Handsome language."

"Yes," he said. "Very pretty."

"This just in: I like you a lot."

And they were about to kiss again when heavy Owen and skinny Carlo sloshed up from the fairway's water hazard to the left, wearing miner's lamped helmets and weedy hip waders, garden rakes and full gunnysacks in their hands.

"Ill met by moonlight," Carlo muttered.

Owen hefted a gunnysack high and shouted, "You guys

want any golf balls?" Pierre and Iona jolted up and straightened themselves. Owen said, "We got plenty." When he only got hard stares from them, he said, "I guess we'll be going."

Sloshing away, Carlo's jealousy overcame him and he yelled, "Don't let him speak French to ya!"

Smiling, Iona got up. "Too late!"

16

At eleven P.M. Dick Tupper was standing in his silk pajamas in the night of his fancy new kitchen, the sole dull light that of the interior of the freezer as he leaned against its opened door and ate spoonful after spoonful of chocolate-chip-cookie-dough ice cream straight out of the carton. When he'd disposed of all but an inch of the pint, he finally found the discipline to lid the carton, hide it behind the hamburger patties, and shut the freezer door. Wiping his mustache dry with his hand, he then ambled to his living room in the darkened house, singing aloud in a good voice an old country-western song by Hank Williams Sr.: "Hear that lone-some whip-poor-will. He sounds too blue to fly. The midnight train is whin-ing low. I'm so lone-some I could cry." Wrestling was on the television. He finished the Falstaff that was next to his Eames lounge chair, fumbled through three remotes until he found the one for the television, and switched it off, singing, "I've nev-er seen a night so long. When time goes crawl-ing by. The moon just went be-hind a cloud to-o hide its face and cry." And as he walked the hallway to his bedroom, he continued, "Did you ever see a rob-in weep when leaves beg-in to die? That means he's lost the will to live. And I'm so lone-some I could cry." Entering his bedroom, he flicked on the Corbu lamp. Arrayed on an Ikea dresser were half a dozen silver-framed pictures of friends, relatives, and holiday good times. In one of them a grinning, fifteen-year-old Iona was squeezed into a photo booth with him, her sunburnt cheek against his, and sticking out her tongue as he made a grue-some face for the camera. Dick got into his wide, hard-mattressed bed still singing, "The si-lence of a fall-ing star lights up the pur-ple sky. And as I won-der where you are, I'm so lone-some I could cry."

Shambling through the first floor of the rooming house and clapping off lamps, Mrs. Christiansen encountered a pensive Natalie at the kitchen table, one hand supporting her head as the other fetched popcorn from a salad bowl. The girl wore red satin pajamas that did not do enough, Marvyl thought, to defeat her female features, but she could just hear Iona hissing *Oh for gosh sakes it's the fashion these days*, so she let it go. She said, "I guess it's awfully hard to sleep with so much going on."

Mademoiselle Clairvaux glanced up and forced a smile. "Yes. I have much on my mind."

"Well, you leave the food preparations to Opal and me." Mrs. Christiansen pulled out a kitchen chair and heavily sat, with an "Oof." She chose and rejected popcorn kernels until she found one just right. She munched with delicacy and asked, "Anything else we can do, dear?"

Natalie told her, "I was flirting just to make him jealous. And now Carlo says he's flirting, too, and I have no idea if he means it or not. And my heart is torn over another and he's such a wonderful man; he deserves a good wife; and I feel like I'm using him."

Mrs. Christiansen was having trouble with pronoun antecedents. She got back to basics. "Well, the course of true love never did run smooth. You *do* love Pierre, don't you?"

"Yes, I think so. And he loves me. Women will always try to have him for themselves, but in his own way he's faithful; he's as loyal as a shadow; and he'd do anything for me: fly here from Paris, sleep in a garage, flirt in order to make me jealous."

Mrs. Christiansen smiled and said, "We have a great deal in common, Natalie. My Bill was like that."

"And we've had so many good times together," Natalie said. "Pierre heating caramel for a crème brûlée with a blowtorch and burning off his left eyebrow. Skidding naked down the giant dunes by the sea at Arcachon. Or just quiet evenings in the bathtub together laughing over the English descriptions he read in *Wine Spectator*."

Mrs. Christiansen seemed lost in a reverie for a moment, and then said, "I feel the need to retract my last statement."

Shoeless Iona entered the kitchen in her jean shorts and green mechanic's workshirt.

"Oh, hello dear," Marvyl said. "How was your evening?"

She felt uneasy with Natalie there, so she just said, "Pretty good."

"We were just talking about the fun that Mademoiselle has with blowtorches and spectators when she's undressed."

Natalie flushed. "Well, not exactly."

Iona ironically told her, "Don't worry. We do that a lot around here. You're gonna feel right at home."

Mrs. Christiansen got up. "Well, now that you're home, I think I'll go to bed." She headed for the kitchen staircase. "You two can stay up and chat if you like."

Iona and Natalie just stared at each other, not saying anything, and then they both frantically hurried upstairs.

•   •   •

A half-hour later Iona was lying upstairs on her girlhood bed, still in her jean shorts and Owen's green shirt, and listening to Edith Piaf stirringly singing *"Non, je ne regrette rien"* on her boom box. *No*, she translated, *I regret nothing*.

Natalie was lying upstairs in her red satin pajamas, unasleep and wondering if marriage would tame Pierre or just make him that much worse. She heard Edith Piaf singing down the hall. Crickets chirred in the trees. She got up and poignantly went to a screenless opened window, slightly parting the swelling drapes.

She heard a grunting noise and looked down, seeing the trellis shaking and shuddering until Pierre hove into view just below Natalie's windowsill. Shocked, she leaned out on her hands and whispered, "What are you *doing?*"

Pierre got a purchase on the window frame with his left forearm and asked, *"Tu vas bien?"* (Are you all right?)

Natalie nodded. *"Oui."*

And Pierre nodded just like her, *"Bien."*

The trellis was giving way with agonizing slowness. There was a cracking noise and Pierre hesitantly looked down.

Natalie asked, "And you? Are you all right?"

Pierre, who was hanging now, said in English, "But of course. Couldn't be better."

"*Bien.*" She considered her wristwatch. "You have now thirty-six hours to decide." She could hear the trellis tearing away from the house one nail at a time as Pierre blithely said, "I am in no rush . . ." She backed away from the window just as the trellis broke free and Pierre pitched out of sight. There was, after a moment's delay, a crash. Pierre whimpered.

Iona's window sash was lifted, Edith Piaf's singing rose in volume, and Iona leaned out on the windowsill. Natalie was posed in exactly the same way in the window next to her. Pierre put on his nothing-hurts face and weakly waved a hand, but for whom it was impossible to say. When they turned and saw each other, both women withdrew into their rooms.

Upstairs inside the house two hallway doors opened slowly. Iona and Natalie cautiously peeked from behind them, saw each other, and ducked back inside. Silence reigned for half a minute. And then a faint groan could be heard in the yard.

18

Sunrise on Friday morning, the hallway doors again opened upstairs and Natalie and Iona politely considered each other and nodded unspoken hellos. Wearing waitress uniforms, both headed for the front staircase, bumped the other's hip aside, and then worked through a silent and apologetic "After you" pantomime before rumbling down the stairs.

Walking out of the rooming house on their way to the Main Street Café, each separately saw Mrs. Christiansen behind them in the side yard, in her nightcap and nightgown and flowered robe, a hose watering her pansies as she surveyed the trellis damage, and looked up and down the house, mystified.

Iona and Natalie hurried their steps.

Waiting outside the café were Owen, Carlo, Dick, and a seemingly hungover Pierre, still in his green "Harvey" mechanic's shirt, his forehead bandaged and his sprained wrists wrapped. Carlo stood taller and smiled as the waitresses neared. His teeth seemed to have been tossed in his mouth like jacks.

"Sorry I'm late," Iona said.

Carlo got jittery and said, "Oh, that's all right, Iona. We're just delighted to see ya. Anyways, morning comes awful early. And you need your beauty sleep. Well, actually you *don't* need . . ."

Owen gave him the cutthroat sign and Carlo halted in midsentence.

Iona got out the café's front door key and flashed a grin at Pierre as she opened up. The four men cattled in after her, and Natalie worried over her fiancé's limp. Carlo was slouching to the kitchen and socking his head with both fists as Owen slid into his booth and said, "Carlo! You'll want to hear this one."

Carlo slouched over, hanging a fresh "Kiss the Cook" apron over his neck and tying it around his nothing of a waist, as Dick and Pierre skidded along the booth seat across from Owen.

Owen tilted forward and said, "A guy in a fancy neighborhood answers a knock on the front door and finds this grinning fella standing there. Says he's out of work, needs some cash, and is there anything he can do around the house. Says he's quite the handyman."

"Why don't you do him as a hairlip?" Carlo said.

"It don't call for it, Carl," Dick said.

Pierre slumped as if he were falling asleep.

Owen continued, "The homeowner takes pity on him. Says here's a brush and some yellow housepaint. I'll give you twenty dollars to paint my porch. You got it, the guy says, and the homeowner goes back to his baseball game."

"Which?" Carlo asked.

Owen was unstymied. "Royals versus Rockies. Three to two in the fifth."

Iona sashayed over with a saucered cup of coffee and put it in front of Pierre. He tilted forward and went for it thirstily. Carlo jerked and fidgeted and went red-faced as he leered at Iona, and behind her was Natalie, sashaying just as she did, and sliding a saucered cup to Dick. She lightly grazed his shoulder with a finger and he smiled as he watched her gracefully walk away.

"Easy on the eyes, aren't they?" Carlo said.

Owen viewed them with mystery and went on. "Well, by the seventh-inning stretch, the homeowner hears a knock on the front door again, goes to it, and sees his happy-go-lucky handyman. 'You done with that porch already?' he asks, and gets out his wallet, hands over the twenty. And the fella says, 'Wasn't that hard with a four-inch brush. And by the way, that isn't a Porsche. It's a Mercedes.'"

Howling laughter and har-de-hars, Owen giggling first and longest. But Pierre was holding his face an inch from the coffee. Owen asked, "You okay, linebacker?"

Pierre scowled at him.

"We got a big day today. Eat hearty."

Carlo headed into the kitchen. "I'll fix you fellas Eggs Florentine."

And then Iona and Natalie both sashayed over, carrying juice glasses filled with the extract of fresh squeezed oranges. Iona presented hers to Pierre while Natalie did likewise for Dick. There were a good many jealous glances, each of which collided with Owen. The waitresses departed. Confused by the shifting alliances, Owen spun around in his booth seat and called, "Haven't you gals got things vice versa?"

Each of them separately smiled.

"Women," said Pierre.

19

Owen's gas station. Eleven A.M. A white Camry rental car pulled in and Pierre hustled out. Remarkably, another Frenchman seemed to be touring America with his family. His wife was holding their littlest child with here-there-be-monsters wariness. The dapper father timorously rolled down his window just a few inches and said, "*Parlez-vous Français?*" (Do you speak French?)

Pierre held his right forefinger and thumb an inch apart.

The Frenchman said, "*De l'essence, s'il vous plaît.*" (Gas, please.) He shot his thumb upward as he said, "*Le plein.*" (Fill 'er up.)

Pierre said, "*D'accord. Est-ce que je vérifie l'huile?*" (Okay. Shall I check the oil?)

"*Non, monsieur.*" And then the Frenchman was astonished at the gas station attendant's fluency. "*Habitez-vous le coin?*" he asked. (Do you live around here?)

In his bored way, Pierre tilted his chin to indicate the house behind Owen's gas station. Pierre inserted the fueling nozzle in the tank and locked the handle in the on position. Children were gaping at him from the Camry's back seat.

With his familiar French as his protection, the driver felt safe enough to roll down his window completely and lean his head out. "*Tu as presque un bon accent.*" (You have a fairly good accent.)

Pierre offered him his Parisian shrug.

The Frenchman held up a map. "*Y-a-t'il des choses intéressantes à voir ici?*" (Are there interesting sights around here?)

Pierre told him, "*Le village pionnier de Harold Warp.*" (Harold Warp's Pioneer Village.) And in a connoisseur's lascivious aside, he whispered, "*Ne manquez pas l'exposition du monkey wrench.*" (Don't miss the monkey wrench exhibit.) And then Pierre noticed Owen's packet of chewing tobacco atop the gas pump and he stuffed a huge helping inside his cheek before he began washing the Camry's front windshield.

Suddenly Iona was leaning on the hood next to him. She said, "Listen. We have to talk. We have to see each other. Tonight?"

Embarrassed about the chew, Pierre was unwilling to fully open his mouth. He mumbled, "*Ce soir*." (Tonight.)

Tilting his head out the window, the Frenchman inquired, "*Il y en a beaucoup qui parlent Français au Nebraska?*" (Are there many who speak French in Nebraska?)

Pierre tapped his full left cheek and Iona got the message. The only French she could think of was, "*Oui*." The whole family fell into agitated and amazed conversation, and Iona asked, "What do you have, Owen's chew in your mouth?"

Pierre nodded.

"You like it?"

Machismo compelled his agreement, though he was in fact hunting a place to spit.

"Listen," Iona said. "We're having a shower for Natalie tonight."

Shower? But he couldn't then ask if she meant what he thought she did. Wild imaginings overcame him and he knew he wanted to see this cleanliness in the worst way.

Iona said, "I'll leave a note telling you where you can find me. Around six check the bulletin board in the café."

Pierre held a hand to his mouth while nodding his head. Iona kissed him on his unlumped cheek and left, and Pierre immediately turned from the Camry to gratefully spew half a pint of tobacco juice and wipe his chin.

And now the friendly French were gaping at him with disappointed revulsion. The father's side window very slowly rolled up.

Owen strolled over to handle the cash transaction, and Pierre went inside to rinse his mouth out. And when he got out to the gas pumps again, he saw he'd accidentally spit on a paper bag of sandwiches that Owen had intended to share with him. Owen got one out and painfully offered the dripping mess to him, saying, "Hungry?"

Pierre shook his head.

"Help me then."

Owen got on a step stool and half-disappeared inside a truck on a hoist as Pierre sort of watched him, lazily holding various tools. On the garage wall was a sign that read: ANYONE FOUND AROUND HERE AT NIGHT WILL BE FOUND AROUND HERE IN THE MORNING. Owen was, for the instant, wholly absorbed in his work. He said, "Hand me those vice grips there, *mon négociant.*"

Yawning and guessing, Pierre handed him some gloves. A dribble of oil spattered his face from above.

Owen, seeing the gloves, said, "Yep, that's close: vice grips/gloves. I can see that."

Owen bent to get the tool for himself as Pierre sought something to wipe his face with. Hanging on the garage wall was a giant white towel that he used, and then he saw, to his horror, that it had emblazoned on it a bold red "N," and below that "National Champs, 1994." With panic, he scrubbed at the towel with his shirttail, but when he found he'd only widened the smudge, he folded and hung the memento in such a way that the oil stain would hardly show.

Inside the truck Owen said, "Romance! Young love! The hectic valences of the heart! When I see the way you two bill and coo, I question the bachelor's life of solitude and higher purpose that my vocation as a vintner has forced me to choose."

Pierre asked, "Which two?"

Owen said, "You two, of course. But then I think, 'Oh, boy, Owen! Can't you just see yourself skimping on the *petit verdot* because little Oweena needs braces?'"

"I am not understanding . . ."

Owen answered, "You're in love, pardner! Whole lotta things are gonna be gettin' by you." Owen pulled something unidentifiable loose from the underside of the chassis and there was a disconcerting rain of bolts and washers on the garage floor. Owen got out of the engine and happily held the thing up in front of Pierre before going off with it. A hammering could be heard that seemed absurdly energetic.

Pierre walked under the truck engine and just to be doing something idly fiddled with a nut on the oil pan. Immediately the oil pan spurted a leak and he frantically tried to stop it.

Owen yelled over his own banging, "Aunt Opal told me all about it. And don't think we humble Husker fans aren't honored you and your inamorata chose Seldom to be hitched in."

Pierre held both hands to the source. Black oil crawled out between his fingers and eddied over his bandaged wrists. "Hitched?" he asked. "I do not know this word."

"Conjugal bliss!" Owen called. "The nuptial bond! The hymeneal rites of summer!"

"I am Confucius," Pierre said.

Owen corrected him. "Confused, my friend."

"*C'est juste*. Confus-ed."

"Well, cold feet's only natural," Owen said. He hammered some more. "And we are going to cure it with one of Doctor Owen's famous Friday-night-infantile-drinking-games-and-foods-galore bachelor parties. Hijinks, jokes, plenty of beer, and sober words of wisdom from some of the least useful guys in a workable radius around here. The whole thing's gonna go as smooth as cruise control on a Cadillac."

Pierre took his hands from the oil plug experimentally, and a huge gout of oil drained out over his shirtsleeves before he stuck his thumb up inside the oil pan again. Woefully, he looked to Owen. He heard something ring off and ricochet from the hammering. Owen muttered, "Oh, damn."

20

And yet, an hour later Owen and Pierre were spiffed up and at the fairgrounds in tuxedos, Pierre's bandages off, suavely walking past the booths and Weird Animals exhibit just as Mrs. Christiansen and Natalie had on Thursday. Pierre lagged behind to give the Afghan hound a look. Owen pulled him along and walked Pierre inside the food tent. Immediately there was utter silence from the forty tuxedoed but, truth be told, farmerish would-be wine connoisseurs and onlookers at folding tables on which wines, wineglasses, and spittoons were placed.

Owen announced, "*Permettez-moi de vous présenter,*

Monsieur Pierre Smith, négociant extraordinaire." Hearing silence, he offered as an aside to Pierre, "Tough crowd."

On a front table were many bottles of homegrown Nebraska wines. Pierre rotated some of them to scrutinize their labels: Owen's own "Big Red," but also "Côte du Silo," "Domaine Diddly-squat," "Chateau Sorta-Rothchildish," "Henrietta's Grand Vino," and "Property of the Googler Family." Pierre blanched, but then Owen was escorting him up to the dais and whispering, "We'd like you to kind of walk us through how a wine tasting oughta go, just in case we haven't been doing it right."

"Sure."

Owen sat. Pierre scanned a skeptical crowd as he poured the first wine into his glass and held it up in front of his face. "We first look at the color."

All stared in a surly way.

"We do not want to see clouds, or sediment, or . . ." He couldn't think of the word in English.

"Grape skins?" Owen guessed.

Someone in the food tent protested, "Well, hell! I lost the contest already!"

Pierre sought a change of subject. He swirled the wine in his glass as he thought. "We can talk about the methyl alcohol. What we call the legs."

"Hubba hubba," Carlo said.

Pierre glanced agitatedly at Owen, but Owen simply offered encouraging thumbs-up, you're-doing-great gestures.

"We will skip ahead to the bouquet," Pierre told them, and lifted his glass to his nose to inhale the aroma.

A would-be connoisseur put his nose completely inside the glass, dunking it into the wine. Watching him, Owen got up. "We might need some hands-on teaching here, Pierre."

Owen and Pierre stepped down to the main floor as Pierre instructed, "And then we taste."

About half the guys at the folding tables dipped their forefingers into their wine and then slurped it off.

Owen said, "And as far as what Jerome told us last month, I done some checking and that's totally wrong."

Pierre demonstrated, "Hold the wine in your mouth like so."

But Owen jumped the gun, saying, "And then spit it out."

A host of them spewed and gushed their mouthfuls. Pierre watched in abhorrence as a burly highway worker named Orville bent with his knees wide apart and spit a jet of wine to the floor like it was tobacco juice.

Owen happily slapped Pierre on the back, "See the effect you're having? We're already better than last time. And we got forty minutes to go."

21

The sole customer in the Main Street Café was a four-hundred-pound wedding photographer who, in the on-the-nose way of Nebraska, was nicknamed Biggy. Scanning the sports page for Cornhusker news, he slurped coffee and went through a half-dozen stale doughnuts as if gaining weight were his full-time job.

Iona and Natalie stood behind the pink Formica counter blowing up bright balloons for The Revels. With the worm of one deflated balloon in her mouth, Natalie was trying to tie off another. Shrinking throughout her efforts, it was finally knotted when only the size of her fist.

"This food is lousy!" Biggy shouted and got up from the booth, hardly a smidgen of doughnut left on his plate.

Natalie was mystified as she watched him storm out.

Iona just sighed. "I can't be worrying about his little world."

Natalie got his coffee cup, saucer, and doughnut plate and took them into the kitchen. And she was putting them in the dishwasher when Dick stood up from a crouch outside and just appeared there at a screened window beside her.

"Hello," he said. Embarrassed, he looked down. "I'm standing in the pansies here."

Alarmed, she leaned forward to see.

"Oh, I'm not squashing anything. I just want to talk to ya. Will ya go for a horse ride with me?"

"But the café is still open . . ."

"You won't get anybody. Opal handles the after-lunch on Fridays."

Natalie looked back into the café, which was, indeed, vacant. She smiled and took off her apron as Opal trundled in with her ironing board and a basket of clothes. Natalie looked for Iona to say where she was going, but Iona had spied Dick and disappeared. A lone balloon floated across the floor.

22

Frenchman's Creek was pelting and gurgling in the background as Owen and Pierre sidestepped among Owen's trellised grapevines in sunshine in their tuxedos. Owen said, "You see here how I've used the classic, double-guyot way of training the vines?"

Pierre gently touched the grape leaves and hefted the grape cluster in his palm like a lovely breast, measuring its weight. "You have very many the grapes."

"Excuse me?"

"Too manys they hang on one vine. She has only the few nutrients to give." Abruptly but expertly, Pierre began snagging grape leaves away. "And you are letting the canopy grow too thick. You are keeping the sunlight off the grape clusters."

"And that's why they're so hard and tannic?"

Pierre, agreeing, tore off more leaves. "The shade is bad for. The grape mold he likes the humid and dark."

Owen, joining in the harvesting, asked, "You think we have prospects, though?"

Working ahead, Pierre said, "I don't know this . . . prospeck?"

"Hope," Owen said.

Pierre picked a pliant grape and bit into it, shutting his eyes as he tasted the tones and inflections of its juice. He was studious, doctoral, then impressed. "We have hope." Tearing away more grape leaves and then looming sunflowers, he finally opened up the vineyard enough that he could accidentally view across the water the saddled horses Shep and Ida as they minced their way down to Frenchman's Creek and drank with equine delicacy. Higher up the hillside, in the loam and shade, Dick Tupper was snapping out with great earnestness a picnic blanket that seemed as red as passion and Pierre's erstwhile fiancée was looking on with fondness, her loose hair softly rippling like Frenchman's Creek on a sultry August wind.

23

Imitating prestidigitation, Dick reached deep into his picnic basket and produced two baguettes, any number of cheeses, ripe strawberries and pears, a Château Latour 1992, and Tiffany glassware and plates. "Wanted you to feel right at home," he said. Including all of nature in his widened arms, he said, "Chez Richard's."

Natalie knelt with him on the blanket, sinking into the soft cushion of grass. *"J'aime beaucoup les pique-niques."* (I like picnics very much.)

"I have somethin' I wanted to show ya." And from the picnic basket he pulled out a zip-locked bag. Inside it was an old journal that he opened as carefully as an Empire butterfly's wings before handing it across to her. With a waiter's screw he twisted out the cork in the Château Latour as he said, "Journal that the Frenchman kept when he was trapping yonder, once upon a time. Had it handed down to me from my great-grandfather. Mrs. Christiansen read it to us in school."

Natalie read aloud, "*Je suis heureux de . . .*"

"Afraid you've got the advantage of me," Dick said.

Natalie translated: "'I am happy to flee an old, tired world, its stomach sour with spite and corruption. In this land I feast on sunshine and wind, wide horizons I cannot reach, skies so full of stars they are on fire. With joy I feel the teeth of ice, the scourging rain, the sun that sears my skin into copper.'"

She was touched. She turned a few pages. While Dick poured wine for her, she translated, "'My lust was once like weather—fleeting, insistent, little understood. In this wilderness I have density, quiet, and meaning. Here I am never alone. At night the wind tells stories. Nor do I lack for books when I can read the changing plot of the skies.'" She paused. "It's beautiful."

Dick surveyed the wide countryside of his residence. "Yes, it is."

She handed the journal back to Dick but he wouldn't have it. "I'd like you to keep it," he said.

Cherishing it against her chest, she said, "*Oh, merci! Merci beaucoup!*" She hesitated. "*Mais non!* It is too precious. An heirloom. You have kept it in your family for so many years."

"Kinda like to keep it there. In the family, I mean."

She understood his implication. She was perplexed.

With some embarrassment at his forwardness, Dick settled onto his elbow and observed her. Natalie demurely declined her head and considered the open palms that were so passive in her lap, as if they were inked with questions that required immediate attention. A stone was nagging his side and his free hand scoured underneath the picnic blanket to find it and toss it toward Frenchman's Creek.

They heard a tell-tale whimper from Pierre.

Natalie got up with consternation and saw Pierre's linebacker build and his wetly see-through Jockey briefs, water swiftly rushing around his ankles, holding his hurt head and weakly smiling in his shame at trying to spy on them. She asked, "*Es-tu blessé?*" (Are you hurt?)

With sudden energy Pierre tore at some fledgling willow trees near the horses. Heavy dirt clods were attached to the roots. "Weeds everywhere!" he said. "I have been taking down them."

"High time someone took care a that," Dick said.

Pierre had no idea what to do with the saplings so he

pitched them to the side and hit Owen. They heard a groan from him as he stood from his hiding place, also in his sopping underwear and not a pretty sight. Owen penitently smiled and said, "We're just cleaning up." And then he foremanned Pierre. "Looks like we're about finished here, *mon frère*."

"*C'est vrai*," Pierre said. (It's true.) And he scowled at his fiancée. "*Nous avons fini.*" (We are finished.)

Owen and Pierre sloshed back to Owen's vineyard.

Natalie faced Dick and knew that all that was about to be said—the hurtful *I cannot*, the healing *Wish I could*—was at the moment impossible to bring up. "We have to talk," she said. "But not here."

"We could meet tonight."

"Yes?"

"I'll sneak away from Owen's party," Dick said.

Natalie was surprised. "Mrs. Christiansen, she is having a party, too!"

Dick went to get the horses. "You know that bulletin board in the café?"

"'Good food we charge you for, bad advice you get free'?"

"That's the one. You put a note there saying where and when."

"When?"

"Yep."

"No. When shall I put the note?"

"Oh. I'll look for it after five."

Owen seemed to have had second thoughts as he turned on the far bank of Frenchman's Creek, for he saw Natalie sorrowfully packing up. He yelled, "But you haven't eaten the food!"

Dick yelled back, "You can have it!"

And like a huge dog, the third-string tackle plunged into the creek and hungrily thrashed across.

Late that afternoon in Mrs. Christiansen's rooming house, Marvyl, Iona, and Natalie were in the yellow kitchen, trying to make ambrosia, but it seemed just a greenish horror with orange, pink, and white things surfacing and submerging as they mixed. Iona went to the sideboard and got out a walnut serving tray and cheese slicer attachment that Marvyl had purchased on the Shopping Channel.

Mrs. Christiansen said, "We don't have to go overboard on the cheeses, Iona. I've never had any complaints with Cracker Barrel."

Natalie was dismayed but deferential.

Mrs. Christiansen turned. "But this is a party for you, dear. What would *you* like?"

"Oh, please. You should go to no trouble for me. Anything."

With annoyance, Iona said, "Well, in that case. Cocktail wieners?"

With matching annoyance, Natalie faced her. "*Melon.*"

"Pigs in a blanket?"

"*Oeufs farcis.*"

"Oofs pickled," Iona said.

She was getting peeved. "Artichokes. *Artichauts à la grecque.*"

"Yuck. What about those whatchamacallits, Grandma. With peanut butter?"

"No peanut butter," Natalie said.

"So much for 'Whatever you want; no trouble.'"

Mrs. Christiansen said, "You don't have to have anything you don't like, child. It's your night."

"*Anguilles à la provençale,*" Natalie told Iona.

"Which is?"

"Eels."

Mrs. Christiansen was holding up at eye level a wooden spoonful of ambrosia. She turned to face Natalie with concern. "Oh my dear. Eels?"

"Why *not* eels?" Iona screamed. "She's got everything

else she wants!" And then she rushed out of the house to the front yard. She executed four different but equally fierce Tae Bo kicks and punches, then inhaled deeply and hurried over to the Main Street Café.

Opal was ironing behind the pink Formica counter while a trucker from Sidney nursed his coffee. Opened before the trucker was an individual-sized box of Captain Crunch cereal and he was pinging crunchies one-by-one off his water glass with his finger. Carlo was hunched at the far end of the counter and was whining over an impossibly complex origami construction.

"What the hell's that?" the trucker from Sidney asked.

"Swan," Carlo said.

"What's it for?"

"Well, place-card holders, for one." He took a moment to sit back and get a new perspective on the problem. He surreptitiously eyed a nearby Scotch tape dispenser.

Opal warned him in sing-song, "Cheat-ing."

Iona snuck into the café through the kitchen screen door, but Opal saw her as she lifted her steam iron. "Iona!" she said. "How's the shower coming together?"

"We're having a great old time," she said. With some uneasiness she added, "I just remembered a . . . thing I wanted to post."

The trucker went on pinging cereal against his water

glass as Iona tacked her note to Pierre on the bulletin board. She waited by it uncertainly for a moment. Carlo's knees were jiggling as he folded down a wing of the origami and hopefully held it up for Iona's appraisal.

She gave it the attention it warranted, and asked, "Anybody been in here this afternoon?"

Carlo scrunched a little as he confided, as if she ought not to have brought it up. "Opal's in the kitchen. . . . Crawfish soup?"

Opal asked, "You looking for someone in particular, honey?"

"No. Just asking."

The trucker said, "*I'm* here."

"Yes, you are," Opal said. "And I want to thank you for that."

Iona left.

After a moment, Carlo sauntered over to the board, unfolded the tacked up note, and read it aloud. "Mrs. C's, midnight. Room number three."

"Sounds to me like a ron-day-vous," the trucker from Sidney said.

Opal ironed. "In Marvyl's house? Hah!"

Smirking, Carlo folded the note and tacked it up again, thinking, *Welcome to my spider's web.*

The trucker faced Carlo. "Which door, you say?"

Opal told him, "Drink your coffee, buster."

Natalie entered the café just as Iona had. She seemed distraught. Opal and Carlo looked at one another. The trucker turned in his booth.

Opal said, "We must be having a full moon tonight." And to Natalie she said, "How's your day been?"

"Very nice. Good. Excellent." She hesitated.

Carlo and Opal stared at her. He folded and crimped his origami. Opal continued to iron. Carlo got the fold he wanted, put his hand flat over it, and pounded on his hand with his fist.

Natalie skittishly jumped. She asked, "This afternoon, has anybody been in?"

The trucker said, "*I'm* here."

Natalie considered him, puzzled but polite. She crossed to the bulletin board and pinned on a note. All perused her. Carlo raised his eyebrows at Opal, who shook her head from side to side. Natalie spun around, as if paranoid, and they all averted their attention. She speedily exited.

Carlo wended his way to the bulletin board and hawkishly peeked at Natalie's note.

The trucker opined, "Time was when a lady had a right to her privacy. Not no more apparently."

Carlo read, "My room. Number four. Twelve o'clock."

"One of them group things," the trucker said.

Opal asked, "Would that be A.M. or P.M. do you think?"

And then handsome Dick Tupper appeared through the front door, giving everyone a pained smile.

Without enthusiasm, Opal asked, "So, Dick. What brings you here?"

"Wanted to look at the bulletin board."

"I gotta get me one of them things," the trucker said.

Dick pulled a handwritten note off the board and looked around as those with him in the café stared. Carlo went back to his origami. Dick asked, "That a peacock?"

"No, it's paper," Carlo said. "Folded many times."

"Well. Have a nice evening, you all." Walking out the door he stopped to peruse the area at his feet. "Cereal on the floor here."

Opal shot the trucker a look. Sheepishly he commenced returning the Captain Crunch, one-by-one, to their little box. When he completed his clean-up, he held up the box, but when he shifted his feet, they heard a small crackle.

And then Pierre walked into the café in his tuxedo. He seemed stunned to see everyone peering at him expectantly.

"So," the trucker from Sidney said. "You got a note?"

At Owen Nelson's bachelor party that night, Pierre was both horrified and fascinated as he looked at the foods: Cheez Whiz, Slim Jims, Hostess Snowballs, beef jerky, caramel popcorn, Chex party mix, Vienna sausages in cans, boxed Ritz crackers with peanut butter pre-applied, Suzie Qs, malted milk balls, mashed potatoes and gravy, French bread pizzas, and, just for Monsieur Smith, escargots. Still in his tuxedo, he sniffed each food item, including the Cheez Whiz can, while Owen, in party clothes, tapped a keg of beer. Hearing trucks drive up, he smiled expectantly and one man after another walked in: Carlo Bacon, Dick Tupper in his finest cattleman's clothes, the Reverend Dante Picarazzi of Saint Bernard's Church over there on Third Street, Orville Tetlow of the highway crew, the huge doughnut lover named Biggy, the trucker fond of Captain Crunch, Bert Slaughterbeck, the winner of the demolition derby, Chester Hartley, who won the Kiss-a-Pig Contest, other Main Street Café *habitués*, and, strangely, the guys in the scuba gear Pierre first saw on the See America bus. Each yelled as he entered, "Go Big Red!"

Orville said, "Wow! You really lay out some table, Owen. Looks like you got the whole shebang here."

Admiring his food, Owen said, "Well, maybe half a she-bang."

And Dick said, "Probably closer to a kit and kaboodle."

At Mrs. Christiansen's shower for Natalie, Chopin's piano music was playing as a variety of Seldom's older women clunked their aluminum walkers along the hallway floor and handed wrapped presents to Natalie. She was flabbergasted by their generosity and she smiled as they said, "Good evening!" "What a pretty dress!" "Oh, I love showers!" "What's that I smell cooking?" and so on. Natalie, with each gift, said, "*Merci*." She said, "It is very nice being queen of The Revels."

• • •

Owen hunched forward in his chair and his audience hunched forward on the sofa to hear him over the noise. "A guy scores tickets to a Nebraska football game. Full house as usual, third largest city in the state and so on. All the fans wearing red. Chills run up and down the guy's spine. Tears well up in his eyes. But I digress. The guy notices that amid the hordes there are thirteen empty seats, all in one spot, with one fella sitting alone, smack dab in the middle. Well, he was too curious to let it go so he goes down to that row of seats just before kickoff and he asks the fella why they're empty. The fella gets this forlorn look and explains that he and his wife—"

"From?" Carlo asked.

"Elgin," Owen said.

"Up there by Neligh," said the trucker from Sidney.

Owen continued, "They'd been coming to Cornhusker games since the days of Bob Devaney and they got to know all the other season ticket holders around them, got to be good friends with them, visited each other even when it wasn't the fall, and so on. But then his wife up and died. What a tragedy it was. Choking back a sob, the fella caressed the seat next to him and says, 'She used to sit right here.' 'I'm terribly sorry to hear that,' the stranger says. 'But that doesn't explain why your friends aren't here.' And he tells the guy, 'Oh. They're all at the funeral.'"

Women hovered around Natalie as she sat on the yellow sofa and tore the wrapping off a box. She lifted the lid on the box and exclaimed, "Hair care products!" She faced the beautician, Ursula, and smiled. "Are they from you?"

"Big surprise, huh?"

"I like them very much."

"Well, at least they're not strands of barbed wire pounded onto a board."

Onetta scowled. "Hey, hey, hey."

At Owen's, a raucous crew was hooting and yowling, shoving each other in various directions, taking off feed company caps and sailing them across the room. Carlo walked in from the kitchen with a paper plate of food that he was examining suspiciously. He asked Owen, "Are these really escargots, or did you just put cat food on some crackers?"

"Hell, I don't know," Owen said. "We did kind of run short there."

Carlo went ahead and ate one, and then shrugged as if he still couldn't tell.

Pierre was standing in front of the television, watching with interest Owen's tape of *The Wild Bunch*, when a guy held out a Falstaff to him. "Beer?"

Pierre shook his head.

The guy said, "It's not just a breakfast drink, you know." And then he flopped onto the sofa and belched volcanically. Pierre sidled away and was given a feed cap by the Reverend, who immediately shouted "I'm gonna mingle with the shlemiels!" Someone else gave Pierre an empty Husker stein, and yet another else dropped a nudie Kewpie doll inside.

The highway snowplow driver named Orville walked by, wearing a T-shirt that read, "Instant Idiot—Just Add Alcohol." Shaking a can of beer and snapping it open, he spritzed foam over Pierre's front.

"Oh, hey!" Orville said. "Sorry about that."

"What are formal clothes for?" Pierre said.

"No, no. I have to even things now." And Orville poured his beer over his own head.

Upstairs in Mrs. Christiansen's rooming house, Opal walked down the hallway, lifting off the glued-on tin door numbers with her fingernails and stacking them in her palm. When all the doors were numberless, she turned and admired her work, saying aloud, "No monkey business on my watch!"

On the first floor, Mrs. Christiansen, Iona, and Natalie were hostessing amidst the chaos of partying women, carrying bowls of food out to the dining room table where a buffet was arranged.

Peering into the kitchen, Natalie spied a few of the younger women spiking the bowl of punch with Southern Comfort. She said nothing about it.

Ursula walked in from the foyer, carrying a formidable boom box. She asked, "Mrs. Christiansen, is it okay if we put on some of *our* music?"

Mrs. Christiansen answered, "Of course, dear; whatever you like."

She disappeared, and then some shrieking hard metal music shook the walls. Natalie, Mrs. Christiansen, and Iona all looked up with pain.

Opal grimly sidestepped down the stairs because of her hip and walked with gravity and purpose to the dining room. After a second there was a scream and the song was silenced. Opal left the dining room, humming.

26

Pierre looked at the clock. Eleven P.M. "The hour, it is correct?" he asked.

Dick nodded and got up. "I'll sure hate missing the end of this symposium, but I gotta be goin'."

The four-hundred-pound photographer, Biggy, toddled up to him, grinning, four golfballs in his mouth.

Wild applause from the others as Carlo yelled, "Four! He got four in there! I thought we had him with three!" As the priest used a butter knife to pry the golf balls out, the trucker from Sidney collected gambling debts.

Owen said, "I can top that; I can top that, gentlemen."

With a flourish he led the way back into his bedroom where he put his hand on one of the large brass balls topping a post of the bedstead. "I can get my hooter around this."

Orville said, "Oh! Can not!"

Owen said, "Can too. And have."

Carlo told Pierre in an aside, "Gets mighty lonely out here on the prairie."

With great strain Orville weighed the gamble and said, "Can *not*," as if for the first time.

"Can *too*," Owen said. "Period; full-stop; damn it."

Pierre was dumbfounded as he pointed to the brass ball, which seemed as big as a grapefruit. "That?" And he pointed to Owen's mouth. "In there?"

Owen said, "Absolutely."

"*Ce n'est pas possible.*" (It isn't possible.)

"If you don't think it's so poss-ee-blah, put some money on it."

Looking in his wallet, Pierre found it empty.

"Was that a moth that flew out?" the Reverend asked.

Pierre told Owen, "I have no moneys."

Owen smirked. "Oh, that's a real shame."

Trying it out, Pierre widened his mouth but couldn't get close to wrapping it around the bedstead ball. He straightened. "If the mouth does what you are saying, I will put the great name of Smith et Fils on the Château du Husker."

The whole party reverently hushed. The two kids with scuba tanks on walked in and the silence was torn by their raspy breathing through the regulators.

Wide-eyed, Owen considered him. "Don't toy with me, Pete."

"We will see I have risk-ed nothing."

Owen said, "Clear back, boys; don't want any fingers or ears lost here."

Pierre watched skeptically as Owen prowled a little and then attacked the brass ball like a python, his mouth gaping hugely. Wagers of many kinds were made, and the party crowd was shouting their discouragement or support. Pierre peered closer, fingering his lower teeth in empathy as Owen's lower jaw seemed to unhinge.

And then Owen did it. Hooked to the thing like a sea bass, he gestured wildly for Pierre to get closer and verify his feat. Pierre cautiously approached, took off his feed cap, and peered underneath, seeing Owen's mouth pursed around the bedpost stem. Carlo got on his hands and knees below Owen and pounded the floor three times like a wrestling referee acknowledging a pin.

The party crowd erupted into a huge roar. Seismographs

in Lincoln jiggled and geologists scratched their heads.

Wagers were being paid off as Pierre fell back against a wall and sank to the floor, where he sat in defeat, shaking his head.

Owen sagged, his knees on the mattress, as the Reverend hovered near him like a cut-man in a boxer's corner. The Reverend turned. "Uh, guys? I think he's stuck." Then the Reverend withdrew a little and viewed it from another angle before kvetching his shoulders and saying, "But on him it looks good."

Soon, Pierre, Orville, Dick, and others were hauling the headboard through the clutter of the gas station's office while Owen dragged along behind them, grunting with each shift. Such waltzing was not easy. Angling the headboard around a corner, they laboriously moved into the garage. Owen was whimpering with a persistence that no one could countermand.

Carlo neared with a hacksaw. Owen's eyes widened and the volume of his whimpers picked up. Carlo said, "There's no other way," and laid the blade against Owen's neck as if he were about to saw.

Owen produced a high, keening noise.

Carlo smirked as he laid the hacksaw blade to the brass ball's stem and separated Owen from the headboard.

But the ball was still widely swelling Owen's mouth. The Reverend considered him and asked the others, "Ever see Dizzy Gillespie play the trumpet?"

Soon five of them were in Dick's Ram pick-up truck and speeding along late-night roads to the hospital. Dick was driving. Orville rode shotgun. He'd called it. Carlo and Pierre were with Owen in the truck's load bed, Owen still pursing the grapefruit of the brass ball inside his swollen mouth. Carlo put a beret on the winemaker's head while over and over again Owen smugly made one humming noise, which may have been "I'm rich!"

(Biggy had stayed behind at the party's food table in order to "clean up.")

Natalie would be waiting for Dick in half an hour, so he was flooring his truck headlong and lickety-split over hill and dale, and tossing those in the load bed from side to side with his racetrack cornering.

Worriedly pounding the window, Carlo yelled, "Tupper!" But just as soon as he did so, red lights were flashing on them, and they heard the *hoop hoop* of a siren. Owen covered his eyes with his hands in a see-no-evil way, and skinny Carlo slumped down, finishing what he'd been about to say: "Take it easy."

They stopped, and a highway patrolman walked hesitantly up to the side of the truck, a hand on his pistol. Silence happened while he perused the scene. An inebriated Pierre saluted from under his feed cap brim.

The highway patrolman asked, "What's going on here?"

Orville began giggling. Then Carlo. And then Pierre joined in.

"I guess I missed the punch line," the highway patrolman said, and shone his flashlight into the truck's interior.

In a failing effort at explanation, Carlo pointed to Owen's improbably bulging cheeks, but Owen's forlorn visage was such that Carlo howled with laughter. Owen looked at him with disbelief.

The officer flashed his light on the faces in the load bed. "I'll say it again," he said. "What is going on here?"

They were still laughing. Carlo adjusted the beret on Owen's head to better the effect, and Owen gave him a wild look, as if homicide was a possibility when all this was over. And that only heightened the hilarity.

"Okay. That's it," the highway patrolman said. "I'm arresting you all for disorderly conduct, including the guy with the trumpet piece in his mouth."

27

*H*andel's *Water Music* was playing delicately on Ursula's boom box and Natalie and Iona were glancing furtively at their watches as Mrs. Christiansen sat between old Nell and Onetta on the sofa and ever so gently turned the pages of her 1950 wedding album. "And that's Albert," Marvyl said. "He was our best man."

Old Nell asked, "Was he the one we used to call Bill?"

And Mrs. Christiansen said, "No. You're thinking of William. William's the one we called Bill."

"And who was *he* in the wedding?"

Mrs. Christiansen patiently said, "The husband."

Iona whispered to Natalie, "I'm sorry I've been such a poop, but seeing you and . . . Well, he's such a beautiful person, and it's made me realize how stupid and cautious I've been since I got back to Seldom. Worrying about what people would say. If you have a dream, you oughta go for it. Even if it seems you're reaching too high."

Natalie seemed inclined to concur, but then Mrs. Christiansen interrupted to say, "Why don't we abridge the evening with a game of charades."

Dick checked his watch as he hurried out of the highway patrol headquarters ahead of Owen, Pierre, Carlo, Orville, and the Reverend Picarazzi, who'd bailed them out. Owen's mouth had been freed of its burden by the Emergency Medical Team and his right arm was slung over his tuxedoed *bon ami*'s shoulders as he gleefully negotiated their deal.

With shame and worry, Pierre said, "But you are not understanding, Owen! 'Smith et Fils' is a great name, handed down for generations—my father, my big-father . . ."

"Okay, how about a compromise then? 'Smith et Fils' on the front and the Husker scores on the back."

Thinking of his meeting with Iona, Pierre said, "I have not the time for this."

Owen slapped his defeated back. "Wealth, Pierre! Champagne evenings! Caviar nights! Pay channels on your TV set!"

Owen, Orville, and Carlo got into the Reverend's old Volkswagen van and, too late, Carlo noticed who was missing. "Where's Dick and Pierre?" he shouted.

"In Dick's truck," Dante Picarazzi said. "What's the panic?"

Carlo whined, "I need to be there for her."

"Who?" Owen asked.

Carlo merely slumped down in his seat, thinking desperately of his Iona: goddess, nymph, perfect, divine, and rare.

The Reverend turned the key in the Volkswagen's ignition, but it just made a tut-tutting sound. He tried again, but no change. "Owen, we have a problem."

"And me without a crowbar," Owen said.

The Reverend considered the crew of patches in his van and said, "I just can't shake the feeling that Charles Darwin had no idea what he was talking about."

A half a mile ahead of them, Dick was floorboarding his truck down a country road towards Seldom. He gave his passenger a stony glare. "Iona's a helluva gal," he said.

"I agree."

"A fella'd be a damn fool not to fall in love with her if she took a shine to him."

"How is it that Owen puts it? We are on the same page?"

"Well then," Dick said, and just stared ahead for a minute.

"What is happening at a shower?" Pierre finally asked.

Dick read his overly interested face and said, "I'll just let you live with your fantasy."

Natalie was in Mrs. Christiansen's rooming house, sitting on her bed in a pink silk georgette slipdress with shirring detail. She stared in perplexity at the many gifts she'd been given: hair products, a box of truffles, a stack of Tupperware bowls, six steak knives, a wine decanter in the shape of a mallard, a pink quilted scrapbook, *The Joy of Cooking*, and three strands of Onetta's hard-to-find barbed wire pounded onto a board. Were she in France, she thought, she'd have guessed she was getting married.

Iona was in her own room, turning in front of the dresser mirror to see the fit on her stonewashed jeans and wondering if a sequined black plunge-front bra would seem too wanton even to a European. She changed into a white silk camisole while humming Rodgers and Hart's "Isn't It Romantic?" The house was quiet, except for some discreet sounds from downstairs as Mrs. Christiansen stacked things in the dishwasher. Iona heard a car door slam and hurried to the window. She parted the curtain.

At Owen's gas station, Dick swerved his truck into a gas lane and Pierre got out. The hullabaloo inside Owen's bungalow was still as loud as a Manchester United football game, and Pierre was heading toward the hue and cry when he saw the Ram's engine was still running. He asked, "Are you not rejoining the party?"

"I'm a little tired," Dick said.

Pierre smiled as he saw his way to Iona simplified. He looked at his Piaget watch but wasn't sure if he'd set it right. "What hour have you now?"

"After midnight."

"Well, goodbye then," Pierre hurriedly said, shook the cattleman's hand in a French farewell, and slammed the Ram's door. Watching Dick head north toward his ranch, away from Natalie, Pierre raked back his lion's mane of hair, straightened his black bow tie, and then walked kitty-corner to Mrs. Christiansen's house.

• • •

Natalie strolled by Mrs. Christiansen's tomato plants, one hand lightly flitting over the leaves, the night of the yard soft as silk to her skin. Cicadas were shrill in the trees. She inhaled the hay-scented air like nourishment. Envied the silence that only she disturbed. Worked out in her mind the question, *Who do you love?*

28

When no one, he was sure, was watching, Pierre Smith hustled from behind a shade tree to the side of Mrs. Christiansen's grand, three-story rooming house and looked at the upstairs windows. All were still lighted. In one he thought he saw a wide shape pirouetting while she toyed with her hair. Ursula's room. And then he thought he heard the kitchen's screen door creak shut as if a wandering roomer had entered the building from the vegetable garden. He went to the trellis he'd destroyed Thursday night and found Carlo Bacon hadn't yet repaired it. He sidestepped along the house, looking up, until he found a gutter downspout. He shinnied up.

Meanwhile, Dick Tupper ended his dupery and headed back into Seldom, turning off the ignition for the final half block and letting his truck silently glide, its tires popping gravel, until it halted in Mrs. Christiansen's alley. He checked his handsome face in the mirror, smoothed his mustache, and shut the driver's side door so quietly it was softer than the crunch of celery at a ladies' tea. And then he crept up to the kitchen porch steps, just missing Natalie as she ascended the servants' staircase to her room. He peeked through the fly-specked screen door and saw Mrs. Christiansen humming as she put away wine glasses in a cupboard. She and Dick both heard a wrenching metal noise as a faraway downspout gave way. They heard a whump as Pierre hit the ground, flat on his back.

Mrs. Christiansen said to herself, "My goodness, what was that?" She scuttled out to the front porch.

While she was away, Dick sneaked in through the screened kitchen door and found the servants' staircase. He took off his faux crocodile cowboy boots and walked up with them joined in one hand.

Outside, on the front porch, Mrs. Christiansen was looking down at the downspout that had so mysteriously crashed. She couldn't see Pierre hiding under her juniper bushes. She said to herself, "This house is falling apart."

Pierre was trying to get deeper into the junipers when he found an open basement window. What luck! Squeezing headfirst through the window, he fell into stacked cans of housepaint that thunked and rang on the basement floor. Had Mrs. Christiansen been near, she'd have heard him mutter "Mmpff." But she was inside the house.

Natalie Clairvaux was prettily sitting on her bed, facing herself and her conscience in the pier glass mirror. She silently rehearsed what she was going to say. She revised it. She supplied histrionic gestures. She changed her mind. She posed differently.

Dick was sneaking from door to door in the upstairs hallway, holding his boots in one hand. All the numbers were gone. He stopped before one maple door and touched his fingertips to the glue spot. He peered closer, as if he could read a faint trace of the numeral. Was it number four? Cautiously opening the door, he drooped in despair. "Closet," he said.

Another maple door opened behind him. Owen's Aunt Opal walked out of her room, binding her terrycloth robe around her, and Dick hid inside the closet. She shut her door just as he did, and then she went downstairs by the front staircase.

Still waiting impatiently, Iona and Natalie both opened

their doors to peek out. Seeing only each other, they quickly ducked back inside, slamming their doors closed.

Crawling up the wooden basement stairs on his hands and knees, Pierre hit the kitchen door with his head, inching it ajar. A stripe of Mrs. Christiansen appeared as she got a flashlight from under the kitchen sink.

Opal called, "Marvyl?"

Mrs. Christiansen looked up and called, "Opal?" She headed to the dining room. When she got far enough away, Pierre widened the doorway and prepared to crawl into the kitchen.

But Opal swooped in. She called to Marvyl, "Did you hear that crash outside?"

In the dining room, Mrs. Christiansen said, "Well, it's The Revels after all."

Opal saw the ajar basement door and slammed it shut with a swift kick of her foot. She went to the dining room.

Pierre was sitting back on his haunches, holding his nose with both hands.

Still holding his boots, Dick eased out of the closet and edged down the hallway, wagging a finger at each maple door as he counted them. At what he thought may have been number four, he stopped and pushed it open. "Bathroom," Dick said.

Another door opened down the hall. Dick ducked into the bathroom. Both doors slammed.

In the kitchen, Pierre was crawling on both knees and one hand, the other hand still holding his hurt nose. He reached what he believed to be the door to the servants' staircase, but it was a full pantry closet. Eye level with the canned goods, he saw garbanzo beans, Jell-O packages, baby gherkins, and a jar of Dijon mustard behind a can of jellied beets.

With disgust, he said to himself, "*La cuisine améri-caine.*" With national pride he pulled the jar of Dijon mustard forward, obscuring the jellied beets, and closed the pantry door.

Mrs. Christiansen was approaching the pantry and saying, "Opal? I hear your voice, but I can't find you."

Scurrying sideways, Pierre opened another door and happened upon the staircase. Going up on his hands and knees, he turned around to shut the door behind him just as Mrs. Christiansen walked in, slamming that door shut with a bang. Pierre softly whimpered.

"Marvyl?" Opal called.

And Mrs. Christiansen called back, "Opal? Aren't we a pair at one in the morning?" She walked to Opal's voice.

Still in the bathroom, Dick tilted his head out.

Concentrating on the hallway floor as if the ship was keeling, old Nell was shuffling toward him.

Dick ducked violently back into the bathroom, considered hiding behind a sunflower shower curtain, worried momentarily that he'd been watching too many sitcoms, and instead flattened against the wall, holding his boots against his chest. The bathroom door opened and, for the instant, hid him. Old Nell entered and shut the door. Completely exposed, Dick couldn't believe the old crone didn't see him. She opened the medicine cabinet, got out her toothpaste, and squeezed a glob of it onto a toothbrush. She said, "Remember to spit this time."

In the hallway, Natalie was tiptoeing down the hall to Iona's room. She leaned her cheek close to the door, listening for a male voice. Suddenly the door flew open, and a surprised Iona was only inches away.

Natalie was stumped for something to say, then twisted a hank of brown hair in a knot. She turned sideways. "Would you like my hair in a chignon?"

Iona just stared for some seconds. And then she said, "It's darling."

"Well, goodnight."

A frustrated Iona slammed the door.

Natalie walked back to her room, passing the staircase to the kitchen just as Pierre, on his hands and knees, shoved the door. She did not see him, but deliberately bumped the kitchen staircase door shut with her hip. Another faint complaint from Pierre could be heard.

Old Nell exited the bathroom, and heard the latch click as she softly shut the bathroom door. She chanced to see Natalie as she slammed a hallway door behind her. Old Nell shrugged at Seldom's new-fangled ways and slammed the bathroom door.

The kitchen staircase door opened and Pierre peeked out, a hand softly testing his abused nose, just as Dick peeked out from the bathroom. Seeing each other, they withdrew for a second, then peeked out again.

Then Iona and Natalie looked out with them. Simultaneously all four doors slammed shut.

Iona heard Mrs. Christiansen call from the kitchen, "Iona? What are you *doing* up there?"

Iona shouted back. "Nothing, Grandma!"

"But what's all that noise?"

Iona shouted, "I'm doing nothing real loud!"

Natalie primly sat on her bed. She crossed her legs. She uncrossed them. She rolled to one thigh and fashionably posed. She reclined luxuriantly, seductively, like an odalisque, but she thought better of it. She stared with wide-eyed expectation at the door.

Pierre crawled forward on his hands and knees, then remembered his Gallic dignity and stood.

Dick waited with his back against the bathroom door. He bent down and worked his stockinged feet into his boots. Confidently opening the bathroom door, he walked out into the hallway and headed toward Pierre like a businessman on an interoffice errand, nodding professionally as they passed. "Evenin'," Dick said.

And Pierre said, "You bet."

Each watched the other as Dick knocked "Shave-and-a-haircut" on Natalie's door and Pierre rapped "Six-bits" on Iona's. Softly, the bedroom doors opened.

Mrs. Christiansen called from the first floor, "Iona?" just as Opal called, "Natalie?"

Iona and Natalie each frantically yanked their gentlemen callers inside before hushing them with hands to their mouths and heading out to the hallway to see what Mrs. Christiansen and Opal wanted.

Pierre and Dick loitered in the two empty bedrooms, uncertain what to do with themselves. Pierre paged through Iona's *Cosmopolitan* magazine, idly hunting nudity; Dick noodled around Natalie's dresser, lifting hair products and perfumes to read their labels, then putting them back down. Each heard a light rap on the door and hurried to open it.

Pierre faced Carlo Bacon.

Dick faced Owen Nelson.

Pierre and Dick hesitated for a second, then slammed their doors.

Reprimanded for noisiness, Iona and Natalie wordlessly stomped up the kitchen staircase. Each paused to stare at the other in the now-empty hallway, then opened the door to her own bedroom.

Iona was confronted by Carlo. He immediately jittered, hit his thigh to halt it, and then he lurched toward her, holding his arms wide. "Oh, you poor thing," he said. "Who needs a hug?"

"Stay!" Iona said.

Owen was scarfing down truffles in Natalie's room. She took hold of his ear.

Wide-shouldered Onetta was policing the hallway with a Louisville Slugger when Carlo and Owen were heaved out. Doors slammed. Onetta sneered as she patted the baseball bat in her palm.

"We come in peace," Owen said.

Onetta threatened, "And you'll go in pieces."

Owen's hand went to his wallet pocket and hauled out a Falstaff. He held it to her. She softened.

Inside the bedrooms Pierre faced Iona and Natalie

faced Dick. Iona said to Pierre, "About Saturday. Did you know there's a wedding?"

And Natalie asked Dick, "Whose?"

Iona told Pierre, "Dick and Natalie."

And Dick told Natalie, "You and Pierre."

Natalie and Pierre simultaneously replied, "*Comment?*" (Say again?)

Dick told Natalie, "You're getting married."

Each said with astonishment, "Married!"

Onetta, Carlo, and Owen were sitting on the hallway carpet, sharing the Falstaff, hearing havoc in both French and English behind them. Onetta got up. "You guys want another?"

They allowed as to how that just might hit the spot, and Onetta went downstairs.

Carlo asked, "You see Natalie in there?"

Owen said, "Oh, yeah."

"What was she wearing?"

"Silk georgette slipdress with shirring detail."

Pandemonium was growing huge in the rooms.

Carlo asked, "She have a pretty shape?"

"Oh, yeah. And Iona?"

"Wore this flimsy little thing. Silk charmeuse camisole over low rise, bootcut jeans."

"Sure wish I woulda been there."

The skinny cook closed his eyes in contemplation. "I do enjoy seeing a pretty shape."

Closing his eyes as well, Owen said, "Precious memories. How they linger."

And then Owen and Carlo opened their eyes. Stern Mrs. Christiansen and Owen's Aunt Opal were in the hallway in front of them, arms folded, seething.

"Or, you can lose 'em in an instant," Owen said.

29

On Main Street outside Mrs. Christiansen's, twenty townspeople were in robes and pajamas, gazing up at the fully lighted house. They heard hollering and protests in French and English. A child asked, "Is this a dream?" One guy was eating popcorn from a paper sack and sharing it all around. Mrs. Slaughterbeck poured hot kettle water into tea cups and a little girl carried them to others. She collected money to help repair her father's Buick.

Bert Slaughterbeck asked Orville, "You don't s'pose it's poltergeists, do ya?"

Orville stated, "It's the hobgoblin company of love."

The townspeople paused to stare at him.

Inside the house, Iona's bedroom door flew open and Opal hauled in Owen by his ear. Mrs. Christiansen grandly entered, and Dick escorted Natalie, a hand gently riding her shirred lower back. When Carlo slunk in, he held his shirt collar high to hide his face, like a criminal avoiding cameras on his way to jail. And then, for no good reason, Onetta and old Nell walked in. Pierre watched the parade with mystification and was about to shut the door to insure that no one else would crowd in when the Reverend Picarazzi crowded in, wearing a purple stole over his party clothes and toting his Extreme Unction kit.

Silence.

Looking around, he took off his stole and muttered, "I must've been misinformed."

Pierre glanced at his Piaget watch and saw it was three in the morning. He stood on his tiptoes to see over everyone's head, and waved to his fiancée, who was wedged between Carlo and Owen. Because of the hubbub he had to yell. "I have only one thing to say to you!"

She yelled back, "What?"

"Nine hours!"

Onetta surprised the crowd by shooting a starter's pistol out the screenless window and shouting, "Quiet!"

Shredding gunsmoke straggled out on a gentle August breeze.

Mrs. Christiansen nodded thanks to Onetta and became teacherly. "Hands out of pockets," she instructed, and Carlo and Pierre complied. "Nell, is that gum?"

Old Nell spit her Wrigley's into a tin wastepaper basket. It clanged.

Mrs. Christiansen delivered her first chastisement by turning to the cattleman. "And you, Dick Tupper! I'm surprised at you!"

"You know, Mrs. Christiansen, I'm sorta surprised at myself."

"Men! On the second floor!"

All the males hung their heads in shame.

Iona said, "We're sorry, Grandma."

Dante Picarazzi said, "When you think about it, it's not so bad, really."

"Syncretism!" Owen's Aunt Opal exclaimed.

Who knows where she got the word?

There was another knock on the door. Pierre, finding this beyond belief, struggled his way between bodies to open it. The grinning trucker from Sidney was standing in the hallway, hefting a pony beer keg on his broad shoulder, in his free hand stacked plastic cups.

Ursula walked up behind him, her orange hair newly spiked, wiping sleep from her eyes. She asked, "Did someone hear a door slam?"

Critical mass was reached when the trucker from Sidney invited Ursula to join him in Iona's bedroom and the thirteen tried to sort themselves out. Owen directed traffic with a bullhorn rolled from Iona's *Cosmopolitan* magazine. "Plenty of room here, plenty of room. Men, stay against the walls! Women on the bed!"

Carlo petted his Dick Tracy mustache as he snickered and said, "Hubba hubba."

Natalie, Iona, Mrs. Christiansen, Opal, Onetta, Nell, and Ursula obeyed Owen's instructions. Mrs. Christiansen got to a tottering stand on the mattress as she shouted, "There seems to be some contention over who is marrying Mademoiselle Clairvaux."

Immediately half the room pointed to Pierre, and the other half pointed to Dick. They felt accused. They shrank.

And then Iona's double bed gave way from the weight, its wooden frame fracturing with a shriek.

Confusion ensued.

Reverend Picarazzi sidled up to Owen and confided, "I think the floor could go next."

Owen shifted his weight from his right foot to his left

and heard an elephant groan from the joists. He raised his *Cosmo*. "Uh, people? We have a situation here."

In the mass exodus, Mrs. Christiansen told Iona, "Let's see: we have Cracker Barrel cheese left. There's still some of that good ambrosia . . ."

Opal said, "I could cook up something."

And all yelled in unison, "No!"

30

Outside Mrs. Christiansen's rooming house, the confederacy of onlookers had doubled in number. Lawn chairs and picnic tables had been teamstered over. Orville Tetlow's wife was filling coffee cups from a chuffing urn on a card table. A girl was walking along and holding out a pastry box and people chose donuts from it. Inquiring minds had congested around Bert Slaughterbeck as he held forth. "Whereas if it was poltergeists, I think you'd see some of that levitation and telekinesis, plus those little red pig eyes and books flying across the room."

And now there was a buffet in the upstairs hallway. Mrs.

Christiansen brought out her best silver coffee service and china. Toasts and pastries were in white-napkined baskets. It looked like a catered affair.

Carlo moonily stared at Iona's room, still thinking, *One heart, one bed, one troth,* and he said to no one in particular, "I just hope she learns to love again."

Owen hauled a chair up to the buffet table and was ravening with great relish as he told the priest, "What I did was combine about sixty percent cabernet sauvignon grape and about thirty percent merlot, plus some cabernet franc and malbec to keep it true to the soft and fruity . . ."

Natalie interrupted to fill Owen's coffee cup.

Owen asked her, "Any progress on your end?"

"Two say I should marry Pierre. Two say Dick. Two say it is usually hotter in August. Iona is abstaining. What do you think?"

"We *could* be a little cooler this year."

The Reverend Picarazzi kicked his shin.

"Oh that," Owen said. "Well, I'm a silent partner in 'Smith et Fils' now, so my choice would be whatever makes Pierre happiest."

And then the Reverend Picarazzi spoke and the river of his sentences was so slowed by his tiredness that she understood many words. "You and your fiancé," he said, interlocking his fingers, "you fit together, you mesh. You accessorize each other, so to speak. And Iona and Dick: peas in a pod. Hand in glove. But you switch the parties around—if you don't mind my saying—it's a shtickl crazy. You find yourself thinking, *What shoes do I wear with this?* I haven't any wisdom; I just call 'em like I see 'em."

She smiled and got up and went to Iona's room, where six women gathered to dispassionately list Pierre Smith's good and bad points.

Iona said, "He's French, number one."

Opal asked, "I forget: Was that a good or bad point?"

Iona smiled. "*C'est bon!*"

Ursula said, "He's a hunk."

Mrs. Christiansen said, "He'll be a good provider."

And old Nell said, "He's always carrying around that duck."

She was stared at.

Iona said, "You're thinking of Chester."

"Oh."

Opal folded her arms with finality. "I have it on good authority that he's a philanderer."

"Oh, he is not," Iona said.

"You say that like it bothers you," Ursula said.

"Are we talking about Chester?" Nell asked.

They all shouted, "No!"

• • •

Cigars made Natalie's quarters as gray as a political back room as Dick straddled a Shaker chair he'd spun around and Pierre hunkered on the floored mattress, his head in his hands, his jacket and bow tie off.

With some heroism, the rancher said, "You know, actually a guy like you couldn't make a better choice for a wife. She's smart, fun to be with, beautiful, and you can tell in an instant what a good person she is. And it's as plain as the nose on your face that she loves you . . ."

Pierre jerked his head up, his door-damaged nose heavily bandaged and no longer noble. "She loves *you*!"

Dick held his cigar in his mouth as he gave that solemn thought. Cigar smoke lengthened toward the ceiling, waving like seaweed, and he said, "She was trying to make you jealous."

"She's crazy!"

Skinny Carlo was stooping to tap cigar ash into a plastic cup on the floor when he noticed the Ferragamo loafer Pierre tore on his Wednesday walk into Seldom. "Whose shoe you s'pose this is?"

Pierre turned, struck by her tenderness for him. "She *kept* it?"

Dick said, "See there?"

• • •

In Mrs. Christiansen's many slept. Ursula was on Iona's floor, a hand slung over her boom box. In the hallway, the guys with the scuba tanks were hugging them against the main staircase railing. Owen was next to the hallway food table on a dining room chair, balancing precariously on its hind legs as he snored. Carlo was underneath the hallway table, jam dripping onto his cheek. The trucker from Sidney was sitting upright against his pony keg, in his hand Natalie's gift of a mallard wine decanter, now half-filled with beer.

Even though it was nearing sunrise, Dick was still awake and soldierly on the Shaker chair, paging through the heirloom journal of Bernard LeBoeuf that he'd given Natalie.

The Reverend Picarazzi was face down on the yellow sofa downstairs, his sneakers off, his Volkswagen van's keys fallen to the floor beside a limp hand.

In the upstairs bathroom Pierre was washing up. Water ran in the sink as he shook back his wild blond hair, straightened his bow tie, gently touched his bandaged nose, and for a long time looked haggardly into the mirror. "*Tu es un imbécile*," he said. (You are a fool.) Then he turned off the water and exited the bathroom.

At the far end of the peopled hallway, Natalie was facing

RON HANSEN

him like a gunfighter. She held high Reverend Picarazzi's Volkswagen keys. "*Allons-y*," she said. (Let's go.)

And Pierre asked, "*Ou?*" (Where?)

Sunrise in Nebraska. The indigo skies high overhead were lightening to electric blue and magenta just above the inky tree canopy and to a soft mist of rose and gold at the eastern horizon. The old Volkswagen van was stalled on an iron-girdered bridge high above Frenchman's Creek as two side doors winged open and Natalie and Pierre got out, their clothes off. Sun rays streaked through the woods and the golden sun rose like something wet and molten behind them as she got up onto the bridge frame's sidewall and then he. They looked down to the sun-painted creek twenty feet below as she counted, "*Un, deux, trois*," and they flung themselves naked into the chill water. They gasped when they broke the surface, but soon got used to the morning cold as they swam. She told him, "We have too many hindrances to our marrying."

"*C'est vrai*," he said. "*Par exemple . . .*"

"English, Monsieur."

"There is this madness in you."

"And you are shifty."

"You have no head for business," he said.

"And you?"

"Bad example," he said. "But you get up too early and put on as music your Fred Astaire, your Gene Autry."

"You stay up too late. And you yack."

"What is 'yack'?"

"*Bavarder*," she said. She halted her swim, put her hands on his head, and dunked him into the medicine of Frenchman's Creek, counting as she held him under, "*Un ... deux ... trois ... quatre ... cinq ... six ... sept ...*" She let him up.

Pierre gasped for breath and whipped his long hair as Natalie blithely floated away. Swimming after her, Pierre admitted, "I'm forgetful of you."

"In which way?"

Wiping his hair sleek against his skull, he floated on his back. "Well, I never think about how you are feeling."

She floated too, her pert breasts rising just above the water, her dark hair trailing out and undulating. Seriously considering him, she said, "Actually, in your own way, you never think about anyone else."

Pierre seemed relieved by the revelation. "But yes! It is true!"

"Wait," Natalie said. She held onto his head and dunked

him again. And then she went down alongside him. And they were all ardor as they broke the surface, holding each other and kissing.

"I'm an idiot," Pierre said. "I'm a brute. I'm a beast."

"No more than most men," Natalie said.

"You are too beautiful for me!"

She smiled. She touched his handsome face. "You will perhaps get less ugly as you grow older."

She felt the tolling of her heart as each stared at the other for a moment. And then each independently went underwater.

Small ripples traveled away. Water flattened. There was silence. And then both of them slowly rose up until just their eyes were above Frenchman's Creek. After some cautious consideration, they raised their heads to talk and Pierre became a hard and terse Western outlaw. "Let's do it."

And mimicking him, Natalie said, "Why not."

They heard Dick yell, "We're joining you!" and they turned to see him and Iona, naked on the iron bridge, their hands linked, their hearts united, and then plunging with screams of joy.

31

The grand ball that ended The Revels at the Seldom fairgrounds on Saturday night became a glorious wedding banquet for Mr. & Mrs. Clairvaux-Smith, and Mr. & Mrs. Christiansen-Tupper. Carlo's feast was defrosted and laid out on side tables, with each course described on little cards held up by origami swans. Thousands of colored balloons filled the roof of the open-air livestock tent, American and French flags hung at the entrance, and a wooden floor was laid on the earth. Even the children wore eighteenth- and nineteenth-century French costumes, and hundreds of Nebraskans from as far away as Valentine and Omaha were smiling as the lovers strolled onto the dance floor and the deejay played Ella Fitzgerald's version of "Isn't It Romantic?"

Owen and Carlo were at a side table in jaunty berets and hunching over the high school gym's microphone. "We see that Natalie and Iona have favored the chignon hairstyle," Owen said. "And both are wearing jeweled tiaras."

"The difference is in the dresses," Carlo said. "Iona has chosen a lovely satin, long sleeve, Queen Anne neckline with a full skirt and pearl-beaded lace."

Sotto voce, Owen said, "You're shaking the table."

"Sorry," Carlo said, and forced down his knees with his hands.

Owen continued, "And Natalie is absolutely exquisite in a St. Tropez model bridal gown with spaghetti straps and a full skirt with a matte satin finish."

Natalie hooked her wrists around her French husband's neck and softly moved with him as she sang along, "'Isn't it romantic? Music in the night, a dream that can be heard. Isn't it romantic? Moving shadows write the oldest magic word.'"

Opal gripped the handle of a white movie screen and pulled it fully extended as Mrs. Christiansen switched on a high school projector and clicked to Biggy's hokey slide photograph of Natalie, Iona, and Mrs. Christiansen crowding into an upstairs dresser mirror as they put the final touches to their hair.

And Pierre shifted in two-step as he sang to his wife, "'I hear the breezes playing in the trees above. While all the world is saying you were meant for love.'"

Mrs. Christiansen clicked to a slide in which Dick, Owen, Carlo, and the Reverend Picarazzi were making faces as they gripped Pierre by the waist, as if trying to pull him back into the church. She then clicked to a slide of Natalie and Iona putting on garters and showing plenty of gam. Opal, Nell, Onetta, and Ursula looked on with hands to their mouths, as if shocked.

On the dance floor, Dick swung and dipped Iona. She laughed and then joined Ella Fitzgerald as she sang, "'Isn't it romantic? Merely to be young on such a night as this? Isn't it romantic? Every note that's sung is like a lover's kiss.'"

Mrs. Christiansen clicked to the wedding ceremony and a slide of Pierre standing with his hand out, waiting for the ring, while Dick, with both his trouser pockets yanked out, pretended to have lost it. She clicked to the next slide. Same picture, but roles reversed.

And Dick sang to his wife, "'Sweet symbols in the

moonlight. Do you mean that I will fall in love perchance? Isn't it romance?'"

In the next slide, Owen and Ursula hefted feed shovels loaded with rice. They were mugging for the camera as they waited for the happy couples to descend the church steps. Mrs. Christiansen clicked again. Natalie had tossed her garter. In the scrum for it, the trucker from Sidney held it out of Carlo's reach.

And now Natalie and Pierre were kissing, and all of Seldom had joined them on the dance floor, Carlo with Ursula, the Reverend Picarazzi with Owen's Aunt Opal, Onetta with old Nell, all singing along with Ella Fitzgerald, "'Sweet symbols in the moonlight. Do you mean that I will fall in love perchance? Isn't it romantic? Isn't it romance?'"

And Biggy crouched to take a gag photograph of Owen seemingly drunk, his head flat on the table, and tipped over beside his gaping mouth was a high-shouldered bottle of red wine that would soon be distributed by the firm of Smith et Fils.

 **Perennial**

Books by Ron Hansen:

Isn't It Romantic?: *An Entertainment*
ISBN 0-06-051767-0 (paperback)
Mistaken identity, botched schemes, and hilarious misunderstandings all play a part
when Nebraskan common sense and Parisian sophistication collide.

A Stay Against Confusion: *Essays on Faith and Fiction*
ISBN 0-06-095668-2 (paperback)
This surprisingly intimate book brings together the literary and religious impulses
that inform the life of one of our most gifted writers of fiction, Ron Hansen.

Hitler's Niece
ISBN 0-06-093220-1 (paperback) • ISBN 0-694-52198-1 (audio)
The story of the intense and disturbing relationship between Adolf Hitler and his
much younger niece, whose mysterious death at 23 has never been fully explained.

You've Got to Read This
Contemporary American Writers Introduce Stories that Held Them in Awe
ISBN 0-06-098202-0 (paperback)
A unique literary anthology of short fiction chosen by 35 of this country's most
distinguished and popular fiction writers. Edited by Ron Hansen and Jim Shepard.

The Assassination of Jesse James by the Coward Robert Ford
ISBN 0-06-097699-3 (paperback)
Hansen re-creates the real West with his imaginative story of the most famous outlaw
of them all, Jesse James, and of his death at the hands of the upstart Robert Ford.

Atticus
ISBN 0-06-092786-0 (paperback)
Colorado rancher Atticus Cody receives word that his wayward son has committed
suicide. But when Atticus goes to recover the body, he begins to suspect murder.

Mariette in Ecstasy
ISBN 0-06-098118-0 (paperback)
The highly acclaimed and provocatively rendered story of a young postulant's claim
to divine possession and religious ecstasy.

Desperadoes
ISBN 0-06-097698-5 (paperback)
The detailed memories of murders, bootlegging, and thievery committed by
Emmett Dalton and his infamous Dalton gang in the old Wild West.